This is a work of fiction. Names, characters, places, and incidents are either the product of the author's imagination or used fictitiously. Any resemblance to actual persons, living or dead, or actual events is purely coincidental.

First Edition

Published independently By Mrs YAHWEH Madi

Produced in partnership with You Owe Me Publishing LLC

ISBN: 979-8-9942383-1-8

Cover design by: YAHWEH BEN YAHWEH

Interior formatting by: YAHWEH BEN YAHWEH

For permissions or inquiries, contact:
yahwehmadi111@gmail.com

Printed in the United States of America

Dedicated to ***every soul*** in this universe.

We are all one.

I see you.

I resonate with you.

I love you.

We are on the same journey,

just walking different paths.

Keep going...

Introduction-

Hey you,

This book is a collection of stories, pieces of life, of love, of loss, and of growth. Moments that linger, lessons that repeat, emotions that shape us whether we're ready or not. Each story carries a quote, a feeling, a reflection… something pulled from the depths of real experience.

This is Part One of a series. These stories are not random, they are steppingstones. Each one leads you closer to the heart of it all… my main story Legacy: the story of Marie and Darnell.

Before you get there, you'll walk through different paths.

A little about me…

My name is YAHWEH BEN YAHWEH, but people call me YAHWEH Madi (yes it's in all caps on purpose haha). I am 32 years old. A Pisces.
A mother, A woman, A daughter, A wife.

I've lived through my share of hardships and my share of beautiful moments too. Just like anyone else.

I grew up in the streets of Spanish Harlem, raised by teenage parents and our families. I won't go into my story in depth, I'll leave that for my future project. I will tell you that life taught me early that I had to grow up fast. I've faced trials and tribulations, learned lessons sometimes the same lesson more than once. But I wouldn't change any of it. Every experience, every challenge, every moment has shaped the woman I am today.

I've been writing for as long as I can remember. Reading even longer, it feels like. My mom used to say I learned how to talk before I learned how to walk... and my love for books started before I could even fully understand them. I remember I used to build little libraries in my room. Writing has always been a part of me.

There were times when life made me step away from it, times when the weight of everything almost silenced that part of me. And for a while... it did. But little by little, piece by piece, I found my way back. And without even realizing it... this book came to be.

This is only the beginning. Part One.

So stay with me because Part Two will be in your hands before you know it!

I hope you find something in these pages. Joy, Reflection, Emotion, Understanding, or simply... a moment of escape.
I hope something in here sparks something in you, the way writing it did for me.

Thank you for your love and support... you don't know how much it means to me.

With love and light,
YAHWEH Madi

Table of contents

The Song Within

"Most men lead lives of quiet desperation and go to the grave with the song still in them." Henry David Thoreau

It was a beautiful, quiet neighborhood, the kind where the mornings felt soft and unhurried and the evenings carried the scent of fresh-cut grass and blooming flowers. Children rode their bikes in loose circles, neighbors waved from porches, and life seemed to move at a gentle, steady pace.

Right in the center stood a yellow house, warm and inviting, surrounded by the most colorful garden on the block. Roses climbed along the fence, sunflowers stood tall and proud, and small painted stones lined the walkway, each one carefully placed. That house belonged to Sgt. Marcus Bennett, his wife Vanessa, and their son, Ethan Bennett.

Inside that home lived a balance that somehow worked. Ethan was a gifted young man, free-spirited like his mother, yet disciplined and composed like his father. He carried both worlds within him. His hands had a way of turning the ordinary into something meaningful. A simple coffee mug, a pair of worn sneakers, even shadows cast on a wall, in Ethan's hands they became stories.

Vanessa always said, "That boy don't just see the world... he feels it."

Marcus, on the other hand, saw something different: potential, structure, direction.

Sgt. Marcus Bennett was a man shaped by discipline. At eighteen, he joined the military as a paratrooper, leaving behind everything familiar with nothing but determination and grit. By twenty-two, he had earned the title of Sergeant, a badge of honor he wore not just on his uniform, but in his posture, his voice, and the way he carried himself.

But beneath all of that, there was a quiet emptiness, something he never spoke about, something even he didn't fully understand. Until one evening at a bar just outside Fort Hood, Texas. The air was thick with laughter, music, and the clinking of glasses. A few of the guys sat around him, already a couple of drinks in.

"Ay, Sergeant," one of them nudged him with a grin, "when you finna catch you a pretty lil' skirt, huh?"

Marcus smirked, shaking his head. "When I find the one who knocks me out of my boots, boy." And then it happened. Across the room, like everything else dimmed around her, stood Vanessa. She wasn't loud. She wasn't trying to be seen. But somehow, she was impossible to miss. There was light in her eyes, a softness, a spark, something alive. She laughed at something her friend said, and that sound alone pulled Marcus to his feet before he could even think. For the first time in his life, discipline didn't lead him. Something else did. They were opposites in every visible way. Vanessa was vibrant, artistic, spontaneous. She painted, danced in the kitchen, talked to plants like they could answer her back. Marcus was structured, steady, grounded. But somehow, they fit. Not long after, they were married. And not long after that, Ethan came into their lives, a perfect blend of both of them.

Ethan's childhood was filled with warmth and expectation. His mornings often began with his father's voice:

"Up early, son. Discipline builds character."

And ended with his mother's laughter:

"Come on, baby, leave the dishes. Let's paint something."

He grew up learning structure but also learning how to feel. But as he got older, that balance began to pull in opposite directions.

Ethan dreamed of art, not just as a hobby, but as a life. He talked about Europe like it was calling him. Museums, streets filled with history, artists who lived and died for their craft, he wanted to be a part of that world. Marcus didn't see it that way. To him, art was uncertain, unstable, a risk. So one evening, after weeks of tension, Marcus sat Ethan down and gave him two options, clear, firm, final.

"Option one," Marcus said, his voice steady, "you go chase this art thing. But if it don't work out in two years, you enlist."

He paused.

"Option two... you walk your own path. No help. No fallback. You're on your own."

Ethan didn't answer right away. He just nodded, carrying the weight of that moment quietly. Weeks passed. He worked longer hours at the sneaker store, saving every dollar he could. Sketchbooks filled faster. His thoughts grew louder.

Then one December evening, standing in the living room, he finally spoke.

"Dad... I've made my decision."

Marcus looked up.

"I want to be an artist. I've saved enough, and I'm leaving for Europe."

The room went still. Marcus's jaw tightened. His silence felt heavier than anger.

"If that's your choice," he said finally, his voice low and controlled, "you're on your own financially."

He stood up and walked away, the sound of his footsteps echoing louder than they should have, followed by the slam of the bedroom door. Vanessa didn't speak right away. She simply walked over to Ethan, her eyes soft but knowing, and placed an envelope in his hand.

"Your father loves you," she said gently. "He's just hurt right now."

Ethan swallowed.

"Take this," she added. "And go after your dreams, sweetheart."

He hugged her tightly, longer than usual, like he already knew things were about to change. That night, he packed. Europe was everything he imagined and more. The streets felt alive, every corner holding a story, every building whispering history. The air smelled different. The pace was different. And for the first time, Ethan felt like he wasn't just existing, he was becoming. One morning, rushing to class with canvases tucked under his arm, he turned a corner too quickly and collided with someone. Paintings scattered across the ground.

"Oh my God, I'm so sorry!" a voice said, light and breathless.

Ethan looked up. Golden hair caught the sunlight. Green eyes, wide and sincere. She knelt quickly, gathering his paintings with careful hands.

"I didn't see you," she said. "My name's Elizabeth. You are?"

"Ethan," he replied, still catching his breath. "And it's fine. They're just paintings."

She paused, looking down at one, her lips curving into a small smile.

"Just paintings?" she said softly. "These are incredible."

She glanced up.

"Almost as good as mine."

Ethan laughed, really laughed, and just like that, something shifted.

Over time, they became inseparable. They spent hours painting side by side, sometimes talking, sometimes just existing in comfortable silence. They explored the city, shared meals, dreams, and fears, slowly building something that felt real, rare, and undeniable. A year later, they were expecting a baby girl. Ethan would watch Elizabeth sleep, her hand resting gently over her stomach. The quiet rise and fall of her breathing, the life growing inside her, it filled him with something he had never known before: hope. He painted those moments obsessively, trying to capture something that felt too big for words. He believed he had found his life. But life doesn't always ask what you're ready for.

One morning, Elizabeth woke up in pain. Sharp, sudden, wrong. She rushed to the bathroom and then she saw it: blood. Panic set in instantly. By the time Ethan reached the hospital, everything was moving too fast. Voices, nurses, doctors, machines.

"Sir, you need to wait here."

"No, that's my— I need to—"

But he couldn't stop it. He could only stand there, waiting, praying, breaking.

The doctor finally came out.

"I'm sorry..."

Those words alone were enough. Elizabeth had been hemorrhaging. They couldn't stop the bleeding. Through an emergency cesarean, their daughter was born, Sophia Bennett. But Elizabeth didn't make it. Ethan's world didn't just break, it collapsed. He sat there, holding his newborn daughter, tears falling silently onto her tiny face.

“Your eyes…” he whispered, his voice shaking, “they’re your mother’s.”

She blinked slowly.

“And that smile…” he continued, barely able to speak, “Your mother loved you so much, she couldn’t wait for this moment.. we love you so much”

But love didn’t make him ready. Grief swallowed everything. Unsure how to raise a child alone, Ethan returned home. The yellow house was still there. The garden still bloomed. But everything felt different now. His parents welcomed him without hesitation. Vanessa held Sophia like she had been waiting for her all along. Marcus said less, but his presence said enough. Over time, Ethan made a decision, a painful one. He would enlist. He would give his daughter stability, structure, a future he could trust. His father stood beside him this time, not as a man giving orders, but as a man who understood sacrifice.

“I got you,” Marcus said quietly.

And for the first time in a while, Ethan felt at ease. Vanessa, meanwhile, found something unexpected. One afternoon, while going through Ethan’s belongings, she discovered the paintings of him and Elizabeth, moments frozen in color. She sat with them for hours, then picked up a brush. At first, it was just trying. Then it became something more. Soon, she had a collection of her own. She opened a small gallery, modest but full of life, displaying her work alongside Ethan’s and Elizabeth’s. People came. They felt something. The gallery grew. And in a way, Elizabeth never left. But for Ethan, it was different. Every time he stepped inside, his chest tightened, because those paintings weren’t just art. They were memories. They were what could have been….

Sgt. Ethan Bennett built a strong career. He wore the uniform with pride. He raised his daughter with love, patience, and quiet strength. But deep inside him, there was still something unfinished, a song of art, of love, of a life he once touched but never got to keep. And though he lived fully in many ways, that song never truly left him. It stayed quiet, unfinished, waiting. And he would forever carry that song within him....

Inheritance

"What a father lives, a son must interpret." -YAHWEH Madi

Two boys. Same lungs. Same cry. Same wide, dark eyes like midnight in a city that never sleeps. The nurse held one up, then the other, and the room got quiet the way it does when something feels bigger than the moment. Their mother, Angelique, smiled through exhaustion, lips cracked, hair wrapped tight like she was holding herself together with fabric. Their father, Marcellus, stood at the foot of the bed with a grin that said my blood did that, a grin that didn't know tenderness, only ownership. He looked at the twins like they were an investment.

"Two kings," Marcellus said, voice low like a promise. "The block gon' remember this."

Outside the hospital window, New York moved like it always did. Sirens. Horns. People rushing with their heads down, chasing money or running from it. The city didn't care about miracles. But that night, two identical sons were born into it. And from the start, they were treated like the same person split in half.

They grew up in Harlem where the air tasted like bus smoke and corner store incense, where summer meant hydrants blasting open and winter meant the wind cutting through your coat like it had beef with you. Their building had a front door that never really locked and a staircase that always smelled like something fried, something spilled, something smoked.

Angelique did what she could. She worked hard when she was working, and she disappeared into herself when she wasn't. Some days she'd be braiding their hair in the living room, humming old songs like she was trying to remember a version of herself before the streets got to her. Other days she'd sleep all afternoon with the curtains closed, like the light might accuse her of something.

Marcellus was always outside. Not in the way a father is outside because he's playing with his kids. Outside like he belonged to the block more than he belonged to them. He was known. Respected. Feared in the casual way people feared men who didn't flinch. He wasn't just a hustler. He was the kind of man who could walk into a room and the temperature would change. The kind of man who shook hands and broke rules and made people feel lucky to breathe the same air.

The twins learned early that Marcellus's love came with conditions. When he came home, it was always after midnight. Always with loud laughter and the clink of bottles and money folded into rubber bands. He'd toss his coat onto a chair like the house was a hotel and he was the one paying for it every night, because in a way he was. Sometimes he'd bring gifts. A remote controlled car. A pair of sneakers too big. A toy gun that looked too real. Roses or diamond bracelets for Angelique. He'd smile when they smiled. He'd laugh when they laughed. But the softness never lasted. It was like he was borrowing gentleness and couldn't keep it long.

"You see this?" Marcellus would say, pulling out cash in the kitchen like it was a magic trick. "This is what the world respects. Not them little report cards."

Angelique would glance over, quiet, jaw tight. She hated the way money could make him a preacher.

"Don't fill they heads with that," she'd say.

He'd smirk. "I'm filling they stomachs."

The twins would sit at the table and watch the argument play out like a movie they weren't allowed to turn off. They watched Angelique swallow her pride like it was medicine. They watched Marcellus treat the streets like a throne. They watched everything. And one night, without even realizing it, they learned the same lesson in two different languages. One twin heard: This is what we are. This is all we'll ever be. The other heard: This is what I'll never become. By the time they were ten, the neighborhood already had names for them. Not their government names. Those came later, when paperwork mattered. The hood called them by what they represented. Lil Doc for Malik, because he was smart, different, already speaking like he had somewhere else to go, and Lil Don for Marcus, because he was just like his father, moving with the same confidence, the same hunger, the same shadow.

And even then, their differences started showing up in quiet ways. One twin, Malik, was the one who asked questions that made adults uncomfortable.

"Why we gotta remember dead people on shirts?"

"Why do the cops always stop you and not the man in the suit?"

"Why you always tired, Ma?"

Malik was the twin who listened. The twin who noticed the way people lied with their smiles. The twin who could read a room like it was a book. The other, Marcus, was the twin who stared at Marcellus like he was the definition of manhood. Marcus liked the way their father's name moved through the neighborhood. Liked the way people stepped aside. Liked the way fear turned into respect depending on who was watching. Marcus didn't ask why. Marcus asked how.

"How you get them to listen like that?"

"How you make money like that?"

"How you get nobody to play with you?"

Marcellus loved Marcus's questions. He called Malik "book smart" like it was an insult with a smile on it.

"Malik gon' be somebody," Angelique would say sometimes, pride softening her face.

Marcellus would laugh. "He already somebody. He my son."

But when he said my son, he only ever looked at Marcus. Malik saw that. He didn't complain. He just stored it. Like evidence & time just went on. Then there was a girl. Her name was Hillary. A Harlem girl who grew up with them like family, always around, always laughing, always acting like she was one of the boys until the day it became clear she wasn't. She knew Angelique. She knew their building. She knew the block. She knew their stories before they did. To Malik and Marcus, Hillary was not just a crush. She was childhood. She was comfort. She was the only soft thing the hood didn't ruin right away. Deep down, she loved them both in different ways. She loved Malik because he was kind. Because he knew how to be a gentleman even in a place that taught boys not to be. Because he carried himself like he was going somewhere, and he treated her like she mattered without needing anything in return. And she loved Marcus too, in the way girls in the hood sometimes love danger without calling it that. She loved his confidence. His presence. The way he made the block feel like it belonged to him. The way he never hesitated, never asked permission, never acted like he was anything less than a king.

Malik felt everything and said little. Marcus felt everything and took what he wanted. And Marcus wanted Hillary. In the hood, you can tell when a kid starts choosing their future. For Malik, it happened in school. A teacher handed back a test with a big red A on top and said,

"You're gifted."

Malik stared at that paper like it was a door. He went home and hid the paper in his drawer because he didn't know how to be proud without someone trying to take it from him. But the next day, he studied again. And again. He learned to love the quiet. The order. The way books didn't ask him to prove his manhood with violence. The way knowledge could feel like armor. For Marcus, it happened on the block. A corner boy handed him a dollar to run something up to the bodega. Marcus came back fast, proud, chest out like he'd just won a war.

"That's it?" Malik asked.

Marcus looked at him like he was stupid. "That's money."

"It's one dollar."

"It's MY dollar."

Their father laughed hard when he heard the story.

"That's my son," Marcellus said, ruffling Marcus's head like a blessing.

Malik didn't say anything. But that night, while Marcus slept, Malik stared at the ceiling and thought: Not me. Not my life. And somewhere around that same time, Malik also stared at Hillary and thought: Not her either. Not in this lifetime. He never said it out loud. Because Malik was the type to love quietly. By seventeen the divide wasn't subtle anymore. Malik had straight A's and a mouth that knew how to argue respectfully. He joined the debate club. He loved the way words could corner someone without ever raising a fist. Marcus barely went to school. He'd show up when he felt like it, because the streets didn't require attendance. The streets didn't give detentions. The streets paid in cash and praise. Teachers called home. Angelique begged. Marcellus shrugged.

"He learning the real world," Marcellus said, like school was the fake one.

Malik hated hearing that. Not because he thought Marcellus was wrong about how brutal the world could be, but because he knew Marcellus was using the world as an excuse. Marcus started dressing different. Chains, clean kicks, posture like he was already somebody. Malik wore whatever, head down, focused. And still, they were close. That's what made it complicated. They laughed the same. They spoke in the same rhythm. They knew each other's thoughts before they were said out loud. They shared secrets. They shared pain. Sometimes Malik would catch Marcus staring at him like he was trying to figure out how to hate him properly.

"You think you better than us," Marcus said once, voice low.

Malik looked up slowly. "I don't."

"Yeah, you do. You be acting like you too good for the block."

Malik swallowed. "I'm trying to be good for me. That don't mean I'm too good for you."

Marcus snarled. "You don't even be outside no more."

Malik wanted to say, because outside is a trap with music. But he didn't. Because he loved his brother. And because Hillary was watching too, even when nobody noticed she was. She saw Malik's silence and did not know it was love. She saw Marcus's boldness and mistook it for certainty. Marcus made the first move, like he did with everything. He didn't ask Hillary if she liked him. He decided she did. In Marcus's world, he was the man. He was becoming the kingpin of the whole hood, and whatever he wanted, he got. Hillary was one of them. Malik never truly told her how he felt. So she ended up with Marcus.

Years moved the way they do in New York. Fast, loud, relentless. Malik got a scholarship. Nobody in their building had ever said that word like it was real. Angelique cried in the kitchen with her hand over her mouth, trying not to make it a thing. Marcellus clapped Malik on the shoulder like it was a business deal.

"Don't forget where you came from," Marcellus said.

Malik nodded. He wanted to say, I remember too well. That's the point.

Marcus didn't go to graduation. He said he had moves to make. Malik knew what that meant. Malik went away. Not far, still New York, still the city, but far enough that the block couldn't reach him daily. He studied law because he understood something early. In their neighborhood, everybody was guilty until proven rich. He read about the system. He learned the rules. He learned how to speak in rooms where people thought his accent meant he didn't belong. And he got good. Not just good. Dangerous. Because Malik wasn't just smart. He was street smart too. He knew lies. He knew fear. He knew what people did to survive. He learned how to turn that knowledge into strategy. When he finally became a criminal defense attorney, he didn't just win cases. He dismantled them. People started saying his name with a kind of awe and fear.

"Malik Carter? Nah, you get him, you might beat it."

He became the best in the city. The kind of lawyer judges respected even when they hated him. The kind of lawyer prosecutors prepared for like war. He wore suits that fit like second skin. He walked into courtrooms like he owned them. But even then, he still carried the hood in his bones. Because no matter how far Malik climbed, Marcus was still down there, holding note.

Marcus didn't become just another corner boy. He became what Marcellus always wanted to be forever. A legend. Marcus rose fast. Not just because he was bold, but because he was calculated. Because he learned from Marcellus's mistakes and didn't repeat the sloppy ones. He built an empire in New York City with a smile that could turn into a threat without changing shape. People called him a kingpin. The hood called him Boss. And behind his back, they called him what they always call men like that. Temporary. And beside Marcus, there was Hillary, grown now, still a Harlem girl, still beautiful, still carrying both twins in her history. She had Marcus's son. And sometimes, late at night, when Marcus was out moving like the streets owned him, she would sit alone and think about Malik. About the calm he carried. About how safe he felt even when the world wasn't. She loved Marcus. But she wondered about Malik. And Malik wondered about her too, from a distance, because wanting her felt like wanting what his brother already claimed. Malik would never admit it, but part of him always grieved that. Quietly. Like everything else. Their worlds collided like they were magnetized. Every time Marcus got picked up, a call would come in.

"Malik... I need you."

Malik would close his eyes like he was praying for patience.

"Again?" he'd ask.

Marcus would laugh like it was nothing.

"Come on, twin. Don't do that."

Malik would show up anyway.

He would argue in court with fire, pulling holes through the case, making the cops look sloppy, making the evidence look shaky. He'd get charges reduced. He'd get cases dismissed. He'd get men out including Marcus who didn't deserve freedom, not because Malik didn't know what they were, but because Malik knew the system didn't get to be wrong and powerful at the same time. He felt an obligation to those who grew up just like he did. Sometimes after, he'd corner Marcus outside the courthouse.

"You gotta stop," Malik hissed, anger and love twisted together. "You can't keep doing this."

Marcus would adjust his watch, smile like a man who didn't believe in consequences.

"I'm good," he'd say. "I always been good."

"You're not good. You're lucky."

Marcus would lean close.

"Luck is part of the game."

Malik would stare at him, same face, different life, and feel that old helplessness rise.

"Do you hear yourself?" Malik asked once. "You sound like him."

Marcus's smile faded for half a second. Then it returned, sharper.

"And you sound like you think you better."

Malik wanted to scream. Instead he said, quiet, "I just don't wanna watch you rot in a cell or worse, I don't wanna bury you."

Marcus rolled his eyes.

"I ain't dying no time soon & I ain't going to no jail, not with you by my side twin. Stop being dramatic."

And Malik hated him for saying it. Because Malik knew the hood didn't care what a man promised. Then Marcus tried to be a father. He really did. A baby boy with the same dark eyes, the same stare like the world was already trying him. Marcus held him like he didn't trust himself to deserve something so pure.

"I'mma do it different," Marcus said, voice low.

Malik didn't believe him at first. But then he saw Marcus actually try. Not in the polished way men try when they want praise. In the messy, real way men try when they don't know how to be good but they want to be. Marcus remembered birthdays. Marcus held his son in public without shame. Marcus kissed his forehead like the world wasn't watching. But Marcus also did what men from the hood do when they don't know how to separate love from legacy. He kept Junior close. Too close. Junior was there when Marcus met with his people. He was there in the backseat while Marcus drove through the city, talking in coded language like lullabies. He was there when money got counted, when phones rang too late, when men hugged too hard and kept their eyes scanning the street. Even as a toddler, that boy had the posture of a child who knew too much. Malik saw it and it made his stomach turn. He pulled Marcus aside one day, away from the crew, away from the noise.

"You can't have him around this," Malik said.

Marcus looked offended.

"Around what? His father?"

"Around that," Malik's voice cracked. "You're teaching him without teaching him."

Marcus's jaw worked like he was chewing his anger.

"You don't get it," Marcus snapped. "You wasn't here."

Malik's eyes flashed.

"I was here. I just survived different."

Marcus stepped closer.

"You think I want him to grow up like we did? You think I like this?"

"Then leave," Malik said, almost pleading. "Get out."

Marcus laughed, but it wasn't funny.

"Get out and do what? Work note? Be broke? Let the hood eat us alive again?"

"You got options," Malik said.

"Because I— because I—"

"Because you a lawyer?" Marcus cut him off. "You think you can just pull me into your world and it'll be okay? You think they gon' let me be normal?"

Malik went quiet. Because that was the part nobody wanted to say out loud. The streets marked you. And sometimes the system did too.

Marcus looked away first, gaze flickering to his son playing with a toy car on the floor. His face softened.

"I love him," Marcus said, quieter reminder than argument.

"I know," Malik whispered. "That's why I'm scared."

And Hillary listened from the doorway, hand covering her mouth, because she loved Marcus, but she understood Malik. She always understood Malik. She just never knew how deep it went. The end came the way it always does. Not with a speech. Not with a warning. Just a day that started normal. It was gray outside. New York gray. The kind that makes the whole city look like it's holding its breath. Malik was in court, mid argument, slicing through a witness's credibility like it was butter. His phone buzzed in his pocket. He ignored it. It buzzed again. And again. The third time, he felt something in his chest shift. Like his body knew before his mind did. When court recessed, he stepped into the hallway and checked the missed calls. Unknown numbers. A name he recognized from Marcus's circle. Hillary. And their mother Angelique. He called back. The voice on the other end sounded far away.

"Malik..." Angelique said, and her voice broke on his name like it couldn't hold it.

He didn't ask what happened. He already knew. He just said, "Where?"

The hospital smelled like disinfectant and grief. Malik walked in like he was underwater, everything slow, everything too bright. Angelique sat in a plastic chair, hands shaking, eyes empty. She looked older in that moment. She looked like every sacrifice she ever made finally came back to collect. Malik approached her and she grabbed his sleeve like she was drowning.

"Baby..." she whispered. "My baby..."

Malik's stomach turned cold.

A nurse led him down a hallway. Every step felt like betrayal. He saw the sheet before he saw the face. But he knew the face. Because it was his. Because identical twins are cruel like that. You don't just lose your brother. You lose a version of yourself. Malik stared at Marcus's stillness and his mind tried to make it a misunderstanding. Tried to argue with reality like he was in court. But no loophole existed here. No objection. No dismissal. Just the finality of a street that always gets paid. Malik pressed his hand to the edge of the bed and felt the urge to apologize for everything and nothing at once. He remembered a story he'd heard years ago. Somebody told it like a lesson. Two sons raised by an alcoholic father. One became an alcoholic. The other never touched a drink. When asked why, both said the same thing.

"Because I watched my father."

Malik looked at Marcus and finally understood the cruelty of it note for note. They watched the same life. And it still split them in half. The funeral was packed. People came in waves. Some genuine, some performing grief like it was currency, some just wanting to be seen. Harlem mourned its king the way it always does. Loud, dramatic, dressed in black like armor. Malik stood beside the casket and kept his face still. The city could not have his pain. Hillary stood there too, eyes swollen, holding their son close like she was holding the last piece of Marcus that still breathed. Marcellus stood a few feet away from the casket, shoulders stiff, face cold and unreadable in the way only men like him knew how to survive grief. The hood showed him love the way it always does. Long handshakes. Tight hugs. Heads bowed in respect. Men who had feared him, followed him, learned from him, now stood quietly like disciples at a fallen altar. But Marcellus barely moved. His eyes stayed fixed on Marcus's body like he was daring it to breathe again.

At one point, his gaze shifted to Malik. It lingered there longer than comfort allowed. To anyone else, it might have looked like anger. Like blame. Like a father furious that one son lived while the other lay still. But underneath it was something else. Something raw and unguarded. Understanding. Regret. The kind that comes too late. In that stare lived a realization Marcellus would never say out loud that if he had not raised Marcus to be just like him, if he had not crowned the streets as legacy, his son might still be standing here too. Men from Marcus's circle hugged Malik too tightly, whispering promises like prayers.

"We got you."

"Lil man gonna be straight."

"Marcus loved you, bro."

Malik nodded through it, jaw locked. Because in his head, he was seeing all the moments he tried to save Marcus. All the times he showed up. All the times he argued. All the times he bent the law into mercy. And now, none of it mattered. Because love is not a bulletproof vest. After the service, Malik found Marcus's son. Junior was small in a suit too stiff for his little body. He looked confused more than sad, like grief hadn't fully arrived yet, like his mind was waiting for someone to explain when his father would come back. Malik crouched down in front of him. Junior stared. Same eyes. Same stare. It hit Malik like nausea.

"Hey," Malik said softly.

Junior didn't answer. He just blinked, slow. Malik reached into his pocket and pulled out something small. A toy car, plain, cheap, the kind Malik & Marcus used to play with as kids. He didn't know why he brought it. Maybe because part of him wanted to go back to when him and Marcus were just kids. He held it out.

The boy looked at it, then at Malik, Marcus would always buy him the same kind of toy cars.

"Daddy?" Junior whispered.

Malik's throat tightened so fast it felt like choking. He couldn't lie. He couldn't tell him his father was coming. So he told the truth the only way that wouldn't shatter him.

"No, baby," Malik said, voice shaking. "I'm your uncle."

The boy stared longer. Then he took the car. And that simple act felt like a new sentence being written. Hillary turned away, tears falling silent, because she realized in that moment that Malik was not leaving them. Two weeks later, Hillary and Junior moved in. The first night, Malik made dinner and the boy barely ate. He pushed the food around and asked for his father again like he did every night, like it was a normal question.

"Where daddy at?"

Malik swallowed hard and repeated the truth gently. Over and over.

"He's gone, baby. He can't come back."

The boy cried that night until he fell asleep, face wet, clutching his toy cars like it was a lifeline. Hillary sat on the couch, staring at nothing, grief hollowing her out in quiet waves. Malik sat beside her, not touching her at first, because grief has boundaries. But eventually his hand found hers. And she let it. In that silence, Hillary finally saw what she never had the courage to name. Malik had always been there. Always steady. Always loving in a way that asked for nothing. And Malik, sitting beside her, felt that old guilt rise. Because he loved her. He always did. But the love always felt like betrayal. Like wanting her was wanting his brother's life.

In the months that followed, Malik raised his nephew like he was his own. Morning routines. Daycare drop offs. Doctor appointments. Small shoes lined up by the door. Bedtime stories. And in those small acts, the cycle did something new. It slowed. Junior was watching Malik now. Watching how a man moved through life. Watching what a man chose. Watching how a man handled pain. The same way Malik and Marcus once watched Marcellus count money at the kitchen table. Malik felt something settle in his chest. Heavy. Sacred. Not just responsibility. A chance. He thought of Marcus saying, I'mma do it different. Maybe Marcus couldn't. But Malik could. For him. For Junior. For Hillary. One night, after Junior fell asleep, Malik finally said what he had never said.

"I always loved you," Malik whispered.

Hillary looked at him like the truth punched air into her lungs. She did not act shocked. She looked sad, almost.

"Why you never told me?" she asked.

Malik swallowed. "Because he wanted you. And I loved him. And I didn't want to take nothing from him."

Her eyes filled.

"You didn't take him from me," Hillary said. "The streets did."

Malik closed his eyes.

"I feel like I took his spot anyway," Malik said.

Hillary shook her head slowly.

"You didn't take his spot, Malik. You filled a hole he left. That's not the same."

Malik looked at her, tears burning behind his eyes.

"I miss him," Malik said. "Even when I hated what he was doing. I miss him."

"I miss him too," Hillary whispered.

And in that shared grief, love did what it always does when it's real. It grew. Not fast. Not disrespectful. But honest. Years later, Malik stood in a courthouse again, suit crisp, voice sharp, doing what he always did. Fighting. But this time, when he went home, the apartment sounded different. It sounded like life. A little boy's laughter. A woman humming while cooking. A baby's cry, soft and new. Malik opened the door and his nephew ran into him like a storm.

"Malik," he yelled, arms tight around Malik's waist.

Behind him, Hillary stood holding a baby girl on her hip, the child's eyes wide, curious, familiar. Malik's chest tightened. A daughter. A little girl with Harlem in her blood and softness in her face. A new beginning. Malik kissed his daughter's forehead. Then he looked at his nephew, at the boy he promised himself he would not lose to the same story. And Malik felt that small, quiet guilt again. Because sometimes, in the deepest part of the night, he still heard Marcus's voice. Still saw Marcus's smile. Still wondered if loving this life meant stealing it. But then his nephew climbed into his lap with a book, and his daughter grabbed his finger, and Hillary leaned against his shoulder like she belonged there. And Malik understood something he had not understood before. He did not take Marcus's place. He took Marcus's lesson. He took the love that was left behind and turned it into something that could live.

Outside, New York kept moving. Sirens, horns, laughter, life. The city never paused. But in Malik's home, the cycle did, not ended, not erased, Just changed. And sometimes that is the most holy kind of survival there is. Not a miracle, A choice, Made daily, Made on purpose. Made even when it hurts.

The Trinity:

"Love ain't always light. Sometimes it's the fire that burns you, the chains that hold you, and the lesson you can't forget." -R.M Drake

Two Faces

He came from where the sirens sang lullabies, Where broken glass glistened under streetlights like lost halos. Where you learned quick love don't live here, It just visits sometimes… then leaves before sunrise.

His pops got buried before he hit ten, His Mama got lost in them same streets she used to warn against. So he learned to be a man before his voice could change.

Raising siblings off pride and pocket change. He ain't have time to cry. He had time to hustle. He had time to fight. But love? Love was a language he never got taught right.

So he grew up with two faces One polished, one poisoned. The polished one wore a fresh fade and clean kicks, opened doors, made women blush with them slick lips.

The poisoned one? He ain't trust nobody Heart colder than them streets he came from, Smile sharp enough to cut through feelings. He said he wanted love, But what he really wanted was control. Power. To feel like somebody wanted him for once, So he'd take a woman's heart, Hold it like a trophy, Then drop it once she started loving too loud.

He ran game like it was survival. Sweet talked queens like he was raised royal, But every crown he touched, he cracked.

Every "good woman" became another scar on his back.

Then he met. Her. The one with the devil in her dimples, The one who ain't chase, she chose like a next victim.

Same as him. She moved like smoke, smooth, dangerous, And she smelled like everything he was addicted to. Pain, mystery, validation, That chaos he called "love."

She flipped the game on him. Had him checking his phone like he was the side piece. Had him losing sleep, losing focus, Begging for a woman who didn't give a damn about his broken.

He'd crawl back to the good one The one who prayed over him, Fed him when he was low. Loved him when he didn't love himself.

Told her he was ready to change. She smiled, said, "You been saying that since 08 ."

He said, "This time I mean it."

But soon as he got that "you up?" text he was gone before the message bubble disappeared.

He thought he was running things. Turns out he was the one getting ran.

She played him like a piano, And he sang every note of her own tune. Cause fire burns, the type to burn everything in its wake. Until, he Lost the good one. Lost his peace. Lost his woman's trust. Now he's just a man with memories, Staring in the mirror like,

"Who the hell I am?"

The charmer's gone, The player's tired.

All that's left is that little boy Still lookin for his mother's love and causing women to feel his pain.

See, he thought love was power, But it was really the test. And when love tried to save him, He chose the lesson instead. Now he walks alone Two faces, one soul, Tryna unlearn the hurt, Tryna find his way home.

She Remembered Her Name

She met him when his smile was sweet and his words were honey.

When he still knew how to say "I love you" without looking funny.

She didn't see the cracks just the man he wanted her to see. The gentleman. The protector. The one who said, "I been through hell, but I'm tryin'." And she believed him.

Cause that's what good women do they see broken and call it potential, see pain and call it purpose.

She thought if she loved him hard enough, she could pull the darkness out his chest and turn it into light. She gave him everything time, energy, prayers, peace.

Loved him like he was home, even when he treated her like pain disguised as love.

Just somewhere to crash between storms.

She fed him when his pride was too heavy to swallow, rubbed his back when his demons were loud, stood ten toes when he couldn't even stand one.

And still every time she reached for him, he reached for someone else.

She kept forgiving. Kept hoping. Kept losing pieces of herself every time she tried to put him back together. Started dressing quieter, laughin less, doubting the mirror cause he never saw her worth and after a while, neither did she. But something awoke one night not loud, not dramatic. Just a whisper in her soul that asked,

"Is this your assignment?."

She looked at herself in the mirror, eyes puffy, heart heavy, and realized she missed her.

Missed her laughter. Her peace. Her glow.

So she started loving herself like she used to love him. Started pouring back into her own cup. Started praying for peace and not for him to change.

He came back, of course they always do. Talking about, “You the only one that always held me down.”

She smiled, but her heart didn’t move this time. She said, “I was never supposed to hold you down, we were suppose to lift each-other up.”

And she walked away head high, heart scarred but healed.

Cause sometimes strength ain’t in staying. It’s in knowin’ when to stop saving someone who never wanted to be saved…

Now she laughs again. Now she glows again. And when she thinks of him she just whispers, “You were my lesson, not my blessing”.

Tale of Lilith

She was no angel But she claimed to be.

She was the kind of woman built different, soft lips, cold heart, trauma stitched up pretty. She ain't trust nobody either so when he came with that smooth talk, she smiled like, "Boy, you don't know what kind of fire you playin' with."

They were the same kind of broken. Two wolves pretending to be lovers. Two egos disguised as hearts.

Every kiss was a competition, every silence a war.

They loved loud and ugly arguing one night, in each other's arms the next.

Told each other "I hate you" with tears still fresh on their faces, then laid together like they ain't just break each other's souls yet once again.

He'd disappear for days she'd act like she ain't care. Post a picture, make him jealous, talk to someone new just to feel like she still had control.

Then the minute he called one "what you doin'?" text she was right back.

They were poison together, and they both drank it like love.

She'd say, "You don't deserve me." He'd say, "You don't even love yourself." Then they'd kiss like it was the last time, hurt each other just to feel something.

She'd catch herself crying sometimes, not cause she missed him, but cause she missed who she thought she was with him powerful, wanted, alive.

But that feeling was fake, just another high they couldn't quit.

They kept running in circles, breaking each other to feel whole.

Tellin lies to sound like truth.

Pretending they ain't care but sleeping with their phones on loud just in case the other dared.

It was love and hate wrapped in the same blanket.

She knew he wasn't good for her he knew the same but every time they walked away, that invisible string pulled em right back.

They were addicts and each other was the drug. She'd look at him some nights while he slept, thinking, "Damn... we really destroy each other." But even then she'd pull him closer.

Cause sometimes it ain't about happiness it's about the comfort of the pain you already know.

And that's what they were two souls chained by their trauma, calling it love cause it felt too deep to be anything else...

They never ended, never healed just kept burning slow, killing each other with passion and calling it love.

Legacy 11:11

"Some love stories don't begin with butterflies... they begin with understanding, patience, and a quiet knowing" -YAHWEH Madi

Before the drugs, before the quiet, before the locked bedroom door there was music. The apartment on 126th Street wasn't big. Two bedrooms. Paint peeling, radiator that clanked like it was singing. But on Sunday mornings it felt warm enough to forget what it lacked. Vicky would wake before the sun most days, even when she didn't have to. She said mornings belonged to mothers and women. She'd shuffle into the kitchen barefoot, twist her hair into a bun, and turn on the radio low. Faith Evan's. Mary J. Blige. Sometimes old gospel if her mood was soft. She didn't sing perfectly but she sang confidently. Like she had somewhere to be and the world would wait. Marie would wake to the smell of sweet plantains frying.

"Up," Vicky would call. "We not lazy in this house."

Marie would drag herself to the couch, still half asleep, and sit between her mother's knees.

"Let's go Head down."

The comb would glide slow at first, then tug when it hit a knot.

"Stop moving." Vicky would tap her on the head with the comb

"I'm not moving ma."

"You always moving."

They'd go back and forth like that every week. Vicky greased her scalp carefully, massaging it with her fingertips before braiding. She didn't rush. She talked while she worked.

"You know you special, right?"

Marie would roll her eyes.

"I'm serious. Don't let these people out here make you small. You walk straight. Chin up."

When she finished, she'd lean forward and kiss the top of Marie's head.

"That's my pretty girl."

There were notes sometimes tucked into her backpack. You smart. You chosen. Don't shrink. At 14 years old, Marie believed her mother was unbreakable. Then Mitch started coming around. The first time Marie saw him, he was leaning against the building across the street, talking to two older guys. He laughed loud. Gold chain heavy against his chest. White tee spotless. Vicky met him outside. They talked long. Too long. After that, he started coming upstairs. At first, he felt like help. He fixed the loose cabinet hinge. Replaced a light bulb that had been out for weeks. Brought groceries without being asked. "Don't worry about that," he'd say when Vicky tried to protest. Marie didn't dislike him. He called her "Princess" Gave her a quick dap, gave her money for school and told her to stay in school. In the beginning, Mitch made Vicky glow in a way Marie hadn't seen before. Some nights, when Marie came out for water, she'd find them in the kitchen Vicky frying something, Mitch behind her with his hands resting on her hips, both swaying slow like the apartment had turned into a private dance floor.

"You my Whitney," Mitch would murmur into her ear.

"I'm your Bobby."

Vicky would laugh, swatting his arm.

"Boy hush."

But she leaned into him anyway. For a while, the house felt like it might expand instead of shrink. The drugs were always there though just outside. Mitch sold. That part wasn't hidden. At first, customers met him on the sidewalk. Quick exchanges, quick handshakes. Marie would watch from the window and pretend not to notice. Then they started coming into the hallway. Soft knocks at odd hours. Mitch would step outside to handle it. Vicky didn't like that.

"I told you I don't want that mess in my house," Marie heard her snap one night.

"They not in the house," Mitch said calmly. "Relax."

But the line kept moving closer. One evening, someone knocked directly on their door. Vicky's voice cut sharp.

"No."

Mitch opened it anyway.

Money exchanged at the threshold.

After that, it happened more often. Then Mitch started acting strange. He went from lively to lazy. From fixing things to stepping over them. From dancing in the kitchen to sleeping through the day. His energy dulled. His eyes sank. At first, Vicky was furious. She yanked the curtains open one morning.

"Get up," she hissed. "You not gonna lay around like that."

"I'm tired," he mumbled.

"Tired of what?" she snapped.

They fought behind closed doors. Low at first. Then louder. Marie learned to turn the TV up. Then came the night she saw it. She had come out for water. The hallway light was on. The kitchen light too. She peeked around the corner. Mitch sat at the table, sleeves pushed up. Vicky sat across from him. There was a rubber band tied tight around her upper arm. Marie stared, confused.

Mitch leaned forward.

"You see? It's amazing. It ain't that serious."

Vicky's jaw was clenched at first then it loosened. Her eyes looked scared and curious at the same time.

Then she glanced up and saw Marie.

Time froze.

"Go in your room," Vicky snapped.

Marie backed away slowly. She didn't sleep that night. After that, Vicky began to change. Not all at once. The singing slowed. The braids grew rushed. The patience thinned. Then one afternoon, Vicky stayed in the bathroom longer than usual. Water running in Silence. When she came out, she was holding a small plastic stick in her hand.

She looked stunned.

"I'm pregnant," she said quietly.

Mitch froze. Then grinned.

"Told you we blessed."

Vicky didn't smile right away.

She looked at Marie.

That night, she sat on the edge of Marie's bed.

"I'm gonna stop," she whispered.

And she tried. For nine months, she fought. The hallway traffic slowed because she demanded it. She chewed gum when cravings hit. She prayed out loud at night. She rubbed her stomach and whispered, "This baby gonna reset me." Mikey was born when Marie turned 15. The hospital room filled with hope. Vicky held him against her chest, tears running down her face.

"He's perfect," she whispered.

For a few weeks, the glow returned.

She sang again soft, but present. She rocked Mikey for hours. She braided Marie's hair slower than usual but with intention. But addiction doesn't disappear, it waits. Mitch slipped deeper. The hallway knocks returned. He began to disappear, not come back for days. Then one day the police came. Two officers at the door. Mitch had been shot. Over drugs. Over something small that turned permanent. Vicky collapsed in the doorway. Marie stood frozen, Mikey crying in her arms. After that, grief swallowed what little fight Vicky had left. Heroin stopped being temptation. It became escape. The woman who once braided Marie's hair still lived in the apartment. But she wasn't fully there anymore. And in the middle of that unraveling Marie met Darnell.

It was late afternoon. Summer heat heavy on the block. Marie was walking with Keisha, laughing about something small. Keisha spotted someone across the street.

"Darnell!" she called.

He turned.

Tall, confident, clean white tee his gold chain catching the sun.

They hugged.

But his eyes shifted to Marie. And didn't move.

"Who that?" he asked Keisha.

Marie lifted her chin.

“I can speak for myself.”

That made him smile.

His whole body turned toward her.

He stepped closer. Reached for her hand like it already belonged there.

“So who do I have the pleasure of speaking to?”

His voice wasn’t loud. It was certain.

“I’m Marie.”

“Marie,” he repeated slowly.

He pulled out his phone.

“I’m taking you out.”

Not asking but telling.

“And who said you could do that?”

She said with a hint of attitude. But she couldn’t hide the flicker in her stomach and the smile on her face. She hesitated for only a second. Then grabbed his phone, saved her number and walked away saying “We’ll see”

And that was the beginning. But it wasn’t the kind of beginning that swept her off her feet overnight, it lingered. The next morning, Marie woke before the sun because Mikey was crying. Not the soft whimper cry. The sharp, desperate one. She rolled off the couch, she started sleeping there since Vicky would sleep through Mikey’s crying. Mikey needed her and all his things were in Vicky’s room. She scooped Mikey up before he woke the neighbors.

“It’s okay,” she whispered, bouncing him gently.

The apartment smelled stale, sour. Like something had been sitting too long. She knocked lightly on Vicky's door.

"Ma?"

No answer.

She didn't knock again. She just walked in, without looking at Vicky she went ahead and grabbed what she needed. She warmed formula with one hand, balancing Mikey on her hip with the other. Her arms were getting stronger from carrying him constantly. Her back ached in a way fifteen year olds shouldn't know. She checked the clock, 6:12 AM. She had school at 8. If she wanted to make first period, she'd have to move fast. She changed Mikey's diaper on the couch because the changing table in Vicky's room was buried under laundry and something she didn't want to look at too closely. She dressed him in a clean onesie one of the few still unstained. Then she stood in front of Vicky's door again.

"Ma, I gotta go to school."

Silence. She cracked it open just enough to look in.

Vicky was curled on her side, still dressed from yesterday. The blinds half shut. The air heavy, she was breathing. That was enough for now. Marie pulled the door closed gently. By 7:30, she was knocking on Mrs. Alvarez's door downstairs. Mrs. Alvarez was older, Soft eyes, Too observant for her own good.

"Morning, mija," she said, already looking at Mikey.

"I just need you to watch him for a few hours," Marie said quickly. "My mom not feeling well."

"Again."

Mrs. Alvarez didn't argue. She just opened the door wider.

"You need to eat before you go," she said.

Marie shook her head as her stomach grumbled.

"I'm okay."

But she wasn't. She walked to school with her backpack slung low, shoulders tight. She had already missed too many days. Teachers had started asking questions.

"Is everything okay at home?"

"Yes, ma'am."

"Your grades are slipping."

"I know."

She would sit in class trying to focus on fractions while thinking about whether Mikey had enough diapers. Whether Vicky would be high all day, whether someone would knock to bring drugs again. She checked the clock constantly. Every minute in that building felt like borrowed time. After school, she would rush back downstairs to Mrs. Alvarez's apartment.

"How's your mama doing?" the older woman would ask casually.

"She went out of town," Marie lied once.

Another day, "She's just tired."

Another day, "She got the flu."

Mrs. Alvarez would look at her a second longer than necessary. But she never pressed.

Meanwhile, Darnell lingered.

The first time she saw him again after meeting on the block, she was walking to the store for formula. Mikey was strapped to her chest in a carrier she had learned to use without instructions. She saw him before he saw her. Leaning against a car, talking to someone. Then his eyes caught her. And he smiled slowly. He stepped into her path casually, like he had nowhere else to be.

"You been avoiding me?" he asked lightly.

"I been busy," she shot back.

His gaze dropped to Mikey.

"That's your little brother?"

She nodded.

"You good with him," he said, watching the way she adjusted the carrier.

She shrugged.

"Somebody gotta be."

He studied her a second too long.

"I told you I'm taking you out."

"You told," she asked sarcastically.

That made him laugh. He didn't push that day. Just walked beside her to the store. Carried the formula without asking. People on the block noticed. The next day, Keisha showed up at her building.

"He was asking about you," she said, grinning.

"Tell him I'm busy."

"You always busy."

That was the truth. Marie was always busy. Busy waking up before sunrise. Busy checking if her mother was breathing. Busy stretching a dollar. Busy rocking Mikey to sleep. Busy pretending she wasn't exhausted. But at night, when the apartment was quiet except for Mikey's soft breathing, she would think about the way

Darnell had looked at her. Not like a kid. Not like a burden. Like something worth wanting. That felt dangerous and thrilling at the same time. The third time he stopped her, she was late for school.

"You keep running from me," he said.

"I got somewhere to be."

"Where?"

"School."

He smirked slightly.

"I'll walk you."

"You ain't gotta."

"I know."

He did anyway. He didn't touch her that day. Just walked close enough that she could feel the heat of him. Everyone on the block noticed, she noticed too.

At home, Vicky drifted further. Some days she tried to function. Other days she didn't get out of bed. The hallway knocks came back. Marie learned to scoop Mikey up before they reached the door. One night, she found Vicky sitting at the kitchen table staring at nothing.

"Ma?" she said softly.

Vicky blinked like she had just come back from somewhere far away.

"You okay ma are you hungry,"

Vicky muttered. "I'm good."

But she wasn't.

And Marie was turning into a woman early. Holding a baby. Trying to stay in school. Lying for her mother. And being pursued by a man who made her feel seen for the first time in her life. That night as she rocked Mikey to bed her mind began to wonder about Darnell, her stomach fluttered and something in her changed. She fell asleep, Mikey beside her and Darnell lingering in her brain. It was late afternoon when he showed up with bags in his hand. Marie was in the kitchen stirring white rice in a pot that had seen better days. The smell of sauteed onions, garlic and sofrito filled the apartment. Mikey was in the bouncer seat on the floor, kicking his legs and babbling at nothing. Vicky's bedroom door had been closed since morning.

Marie hadn't knocked. She already knew. Then a soft knock hit the apartment door. Not the hurried tap of a dealer, a steady knock. She froze for a second. Then walked over and cracked it open just enough. Darnell stood there holding some grocery bags and a small can of formula tucked under his arm.

"Thought you might need this," he said casually.

Her chest tightened. She hadn't told anyone she was running low. She stepped aside.

"Just the kitchen," she said quickly.

He nodded once and walked in. The apartment looked smaller with him inside.

He set the bag on the counter and glanced around quietly. His eyes lingered on the closed bedroom door for half a second but he didn't ask.

"What you making?" he asked instead.

"Steak."

He raised an eyebrow.

“For real?”

She shrugged.

“It was on sale.”

He leaned against the counter, watching her move. The way she flipped the steak. The way she checked the rice without burning herself.

“You cook like that all the time?”

“A girl gotta eat,” she replied.

He smirked at that. She plated the food simply. White rice. Beans. Steak sliced thin with sautéed onions on top. A piece of bread on the side. She hesitated for a second. Then cut off a small piece and held it toward him.

“Try it.”

He stepped closer. Took the fork from her hand instead of the plate. Held her eyes while he tasted it, he chewed slow, then shook his head once.

“Yeah,” he said softly. “You different.”

She rolled her eyes.

“It’s just food.”

“It ain’t just food.”

“Oh hush she smiled, Here let me serve you”

Marie got up and fixed him a plate, served him like she wasn’t new to this.

He looked at her differently after that.. Not just like she was pretty.

Like she was capable.

They sat at the tiny kitchen table while Mikey babbled between them.

“So,” he said, resting his forearms on the table belly full. “Tell me about you.”

She stiffened slightly.

“What you wanna know?”

“Everything.”

She snorted lightly.

“That’s dramatic.”

He smiled.

“Start small then.”

She shrugged.

“Never knew my dad.”

His expression shifted slightly but not in pity.

“Just me and my mom.”

That part was true. She didn’t say more. Didn’t mention the locked bedroom. Didn’t mention the spoon. Didn’t mention the hallway knocks.

He nodded slowly.

“How’s your mom? I used to see her around,” he said casually. “Haven’t seen her lately.”

Marie’s jaw tightened for half a second. “She works a lot,” she replied quickly. “Barely home.”

He didn't challenge it, he already knew. He had seen Vicky on the block with Mitch.

Seen the decline, seen the traffic. But he let Marie believe he didn't know.

He leaned back in his chair.

"You shouldn't have to carry everything."

She shrugged again.

"I'm used to it."

He watched her closely. And something in his eyes shifted from curiosity to intention. He stood up slowly.

"I'm still taking you out."

She hesitated.

"You don't even know me."

"I know enough."

She looked toward the bedroom door, silence. Then back at him.

"When?"

"Tomorrow night."

She thought about Mikey, about Vicky, about school, about being tired. And about how good it felt to sit at a table with someone who looked at her like she wasn't drowning.

"Fine, pick me up at 7" she said quietly.

He smiled like he had just won something. The next night, Keisha came over. Keisha was seventeen. Louder, more confident. Already living a little faster than Marie.

"You sure?" Keisha asked, bouncing Mikey gently.

"He just gonna go to sleep," Marie said.

She stood in front of the cracked mirror for longer than usual. She didn't have much to choose from. But she picked the cleanest closest to sexy outfit she had. When Darnell pulled up the block noticed, of course they did he was young, only 18 but he was big in their neighborhood. He stepped out of the car when he saw her. Opened the passenger door. Not because he had to, but because he wanted to. The ride was quiet at first, the radio played low.

"You nervous?" he asked.

"No."

He smirked.

"Liar."

She crossed her arms.

"Where we going?"

"You'll see."

He drove past their usual corners. Past the noise toward a quieter part of the city where lights reflected off windows and things looked a little less worn. They ended up at a small little restaurant. Nothing too fancy. But not the chicken spot either and something she wasn't use to. He pulled out her chair. Ordered for both of them without asking but somehow picked exactly what she would've chosen. They talked for hours. About nothing. About everything. He told her about growing up with an addict mother too after she told him the truth about Vicky. Not detailed, just enough.

"Had to grow up quick," he said.

She nodded.

"I know the feeling."

He watched her when she spoke. not distracted, not scanning the room but Focused. That intensity felt grown, maybe too grown. But in their world, girls didn't get to stay children long. When he drove her home, the streets were live, the city never sleeps. He parked but didn't turn the engine off. She reached for the door, he touched her wrist gently.

"Marie."

The way he said her name made her stomach flip. She turned toward him. He leaned in slowly. Not rushed or careless. His hand came up to her jaw then he kissed her with intention. Not sloppy, not innocent but controlled. He didn't push further, he didn't rush.

He pulled back just enough to look at her.

"You too young for me," he murmured softly.

"But somehow you understand this life, you understand pain"

Her heart pounded so loud she was sure he could hear it.

She nodded slightly.

"I'm old enough, I'm sixteen, you're only two years older than me."

And that was the night everything shifted. It didn't feel dramatic while it was happening, it felt calm. After that kiss in the car, Marie slipped back upstairs like she was carrying something fragile inside her chest. Keisha was stretched across the couch half asleep, Mikey curled against her chest with his tiny fist wrapped in her shirt.

"How was it?" Keisha mumbled without opening her eyes.

Marie didn't answer right away. She just stood there, touching her lips lightly.

"...good," she whispered.

Keisha smiled without waking fully.

"Told you."

That night Marie lay awake long after everyone else slept. The apartment was still except for Mikey's soft breathing and the distant hum of traffic and people outside. She replayed everything. The way Darnell had looked at her, the way he listened, the way he said her name. No one had ever looked at her like that before. After that, he started showing up more. Not suddenly but Gradually. At first it was just once every couple days a knock at the door, a quiet "you decent?" before stepping inside. Always respectful and calm. Sometimes he came with groceries, Sometimes diapers, sometimes nothing at all but he never barged past the kitchen. He never asked questions about the closed bedroom door. Never made her feel embarrassed about the things he clearly noticed and he noticed everything.

"You ain't eat all day?" he asked one afternoon hearing her stomach growl while watching her stir a pot.

"I'm cooking now."

"That ain't what I asked."

She rolled her eyes but grabbed a plate. He sat at the tiny table like he belonged there, watching her move around the kitchen like it was a show he didn't want to miss.

"You always take care of everybody else first?" he asked.

"Somebody gotta," she said.

He didn't answer. But something in his expression softened. Mikey loved him almost immediately. Babies can sense energy before words. Mikey would kick his legs when Darnell walked in, reaching for him with open hands. Darnell would lift him high in the air like he weighed nothing.

"What's up, lil man," he'd murmur.

And Mikey would giggle like the sound lived in his bones. The first time Darnell changed his diaper without being asked, Marie stared.

"You don't gotta do that."

He shrugged.

"Ain't hard."

It wasn't a big moment. But it stayed with her because nobody had ever stepped in like that before. Weeks blurred together, school in the mornings when she could make it. Mrs. Alvarez watching Mikey downstairs. Excuses for her mother, cooking at night and Darnell stopping by. Life started forming a rhythm that almost felt... stable. He fixed things without announcing it. The loose cabinet hinge stopped squeaking, the faucet stopped dripping. The hallway light outside their door suddenly worked again. Marie never saw him do it. Things were just... fixed she suspected while she was at school or while cooking. One evening she noticed the fridge was full when she hadn't gone shopping. She didn't ask but she knew. Sometimes he'd sit at the table while she cooked and just watch her.

"You like that," she said once, not looking up.

"Like what?"

"Watching me."

He leaned back in the chair slightly.

"Yeah."

She glanced at him.

"Why?"

He held her gaze.

"'Cause you don't even know how strong you are."

Her chest tightened in a way she didn't understand.

No one had ever called her strong before. They called her responsible, mature, helpful. But not strong. A couple weeks after their first date, the closeness between them shifted again. Not suddenly but naturally. The way he touched her hand when passing something. The way his thumb brushed her wrist without thinking. The way she stopped pulling away. That night was the night she decided to give him all of her. He sat low on the couch, one arm stretched across the backrest, thumb tapping slow against the cushion while the blue light flickered across his face. Harlem noise floated through the cracked window distant, somebody arguing down the block, a siren echoing through the streets. Regular soundtrack, home.

Then her door creaked. His eyes slid over before his head even turned. She stepped out wearing nothing but that oversized T-shirt his T-shirt the hem brushing high on her thighs, bare legs glowing warm under the apartment light, hair loose, lips soft. Like she wasn't trying at all… which made it worse. His gaze dragged slow first to her ankles, calves, thighs, hips then her beautiful freckled face. He was Hungry, and not for her cooking.

"Yo…" he murmured, voice low, rougher than before. "You tryna start somethin' or you just walk around like that casually now?"

She didn't answer right away. Just walked toward him, slow, steady, like she knew exactly what she was doing. Every step made his jaw tighten a little more. She stopped in front of him.

He leaned back, eyes lifting up her body again, unashamed just appreciating. "You dangerous tonight," he muttered. "Real dangerous."

She tilted her head, soft smile playing at her lips. "Maybe."

His tongue ran over his bottom lip. "Maybe?"

Instead of answering, she climbed onto him.

One knee on either side of his hips. Hands settling on his shoulders. Close enough now that he could feel the warmth of her skin through the thin cotton.

His hands hovered at her waist but didn't grab yet. Didn't trust himself.

"Hold up," he said quietly, searching her face. "You sure?"

She nodded once.

"Don't nod," he murmured. "Say it."

Her fingers slid into the back of his hair, voice barely above a whisper. "I'm sure."

His eyes darkened, but he still didn't move. "You ain't doing this just for me, right?"

She leaned closer until her lips brushed his. "No."

"Not 'cause you bored?"

"No."

"Not 'cause you think I want you to?"

She smiled against his mouth. "I know you want me."

That did something to him.

His grip tightened at her waist, fingers finally pressing into her sides. "Yeah," he breathed. "I do."

She kissed him slow, soft, like she was tasting him instead of rushing him. He stayed still for half a second, letting her lead, letting her show him she meant it. Then his restraint snapped. His hands slid up her back, firm now, pulling her closer, chest to chest. He kissed her deeper, slower, like he had all night but none of the patience. Like he'd been starving and she finally sat down in front of him.

"Mm," she moaned against his lips.

He smirked slightly. "That sound right there?" he said huskily. "That's my favorite one."

She laughed softly, breath warm on his mouth. "You talk too much."

"Yeah?" His nose brushed hers. "You gon' make me stop?"

She kissed him again instead of answering. That was permission. His hands slid down her thighs, gripping them, lifting her just enough so she settled heavier in his lap. His voice dropped low, Harlem rough with affection and heat tangled together.

"Aight then," he murmured. "Don't start what you can't handle, ma."

Her eyes sparkled. "Who said I can't?"

He grinned slow, dangerous. "Oh, I like that."

His forehead pressed to hers for a second, breath mixing, tension thick and warm between them.

"Last chance," he whispered. "You sure?"

She nodded, lips brushing his again. "I'm positive."

That was all he needed. His hunger didn't rush it rolled in steady, certain, confident as his hands traced her like he'd memorized her already and still wanted to study every line again. He lifted her up, gliding over to her room and the TV kept playing to an empty living room. Afterward, she lay with her head against his chest listening to his heartbeat, feeling like she had stepped into a future she didn't fully understand yet. He kissed her forehead.

"You mine," he murmured softly.

And instead of fear... She felt protected. She felt like she was important in the way only first times feel when you believe you're safe. When you believe you're chosen. When you believe someone sees you and wants only you. For a long time after that, things were good. Not perfect, but good enough to believe in. Darnell came around so often the neighbors stopped asking who he was. Mrs. Alvarez started handing Mikey to him without hesitation when Marie came home from school.

"You got help now," she said one afternoon, almost approving.

Marie nodded because finally she did. At night, when Vicky stayed locked away in her room, the apartment didn't feel as empty anymore. Because Darnell filled the space she left behind and that's how it began. Not with chaos not with fear but with warmth. Which is why Marie didn't notice how deeply he had already rooted himself into her life... until much later. Days started disappearing before Vicky did. At first it was small absences. An afternoon gone. A night that stretched into morning. A morning that stretched into evening. Marie would wake up, knock on her mother's door, and get no answer. The first few times it happened she panicked, checked the hallway, checked the stairwell, checked outside barefoot with Mikey balanced on her hip. Later, she stopped checking. She'd just sigh, shift Mikey higher on her hip, and start the day anyway.

By then, she already knew how the pattern went. Vicky would vanish for a day or two… sometimes longer. Then she'd come back like nothing had happened same clothes, same tired eyes, same restless energy under her skin moving through the apartment like she still owned it but didn't really live there. She never came back to stay. She came back when she needed something. Sometimes food, sometimes sleep but most times money. The first time she asked, she stood in the kitchen doorway, arms folded tight across her chest like she was cold even though it was warm.

"Marie," she said.

Marie was at the stove stirring beans with one hand while bouncing Mikey with the other, she didn't turn.

"What."

Vicky shifted her weight.

"You got some of that money?"

Marie's jaw tightened.

The disability checks started last year. Small payments that technically belonged to Vicky, but she'd told Marie to keep them since she was the one running the house anyway.

Now she asked for it when she needed something. Marie knew what that something was and she hated it. But she also knew it wasn't really hers. She set the spoon down slowly.

"How much."

"Just a little."

She always said that.

Just a little.

Marie reached into the envelope tucked above the fridge and pulled out a few bills. She held them out without looking at her. Vicky took them quick. Didn't say thank you, didn't say sorry. Just nodded once and left again, the door closing behind her while Mikey babbled.

The beans kept simmering. Marie stood there staring at the empty doorway long after her mother was gone. Later that night Darnell saw Vicky outside copping drugs. When he got home he kissed Marie and Mikey then sat down at the kitchen table..

"You gave her money again," he said, not asking.

Marie shrugged, still folding laundry.

"It's hers."

He shook his head once.

"Nah. You the one taking care of everything. That's yours."

She didn't answer.

He stepped closer.

"You don't gotta give her nothing," he said quietly. "I got you, I got Mikey you ain't gotta worry about nothing but you still don't need to give her nothing, save it."

He said it like a promise and he meant it, that was the scary part. Because he kept proving it. Groceries showed up, bills stayed paid, Mikey had diapers. The lights stayed on and the more he filled the gaps Vicky left behind… the less Marie felt like she needed her mother at all.

Time passed like that. School when she could make it. Cooking, cleaning, parenting, Wifeing. Darnell coming and going like he belonged there and Vicky drifting in and out like a ghost who only returned for supplies. Marie stopped watching the door. Stopped waiting for it to open. Stopped caring if it did until the day it did. Vicky hadn't been home in almost three weeks. Marie barely noticed anymore. She was in the kitchen again always in the kitchen slicing onions while Mikey sat on the floor playing with his toys. The door creaked open behind her, Marie didn't turn. She assumed it was Darnell.

"Hey baby" she said.

No answer.

Something in the air felt different. She glanced over her shoulder. Vicky stood in the doorway. Hair tangled, eyes dull clothes stained and wrinkled like she'd slept in them for days. Marie's gaze slid over her automatically the way you look at something without really seeing it. Then it caught her gaze.

She Paused, Returned, her eyes narrowed. Vicky's shirt hung differently. Not loose, not flat but rounded. Marie stared, her stomach tightened. Her voice came out sharp before she could stop it.

"...You serious right now?"

Vicky blinked slowly.

"What?"

Marie turned fully now, knife still in her hand but hanging limp at her side.

"You serious?" she repeated, louder. "You really walking in here pregnant!"

Silence filled the kitchen.

Mikey kept playing.

Vicky's expression shifted annoyance first, then defensiveness.

"It ain't your business."

Marie let out a short laugh that held no humor.

"Ain't my business?"

Her chest started rising faster.

"Ain't my business?" she repeated. "You gone for weeks, come back strung out every time, and now you pregnant and it ain't my business?"

"Lower your voice," Vicky muttered.

"No."

The word came out harder than she expected.

"No, I'm not lowering nothing. You got a baby already you don't even take care of and you out here making another one?"

Vicky's jaw tightened.

"I ain't ask you for no opinion."

"Yeah well you didn't ask me to raise the first one either but here we are."

The words landed heavy. For a second, neither of them spoke.

Then Vicky scoffed and moved past her toward the counter like the conversation was over.

"You doing too much," she said flatly.

Marie stared at her.

Something hot burned behind her ribs. She realized then with a clarity that scared her that she wasn't just angry. She was tired,

tired of being the parent, the responsible one, tired of watching her mother choose everything except them. Her voice dropped.

"How far."

Vicky didn't answer.

Marie stepped closer.

"How far!"

A pause.

"...Couple months."

Marie's stomach dropped.

Her mind raced.

Couple months.

So she missed it last time? Had she been so busy surviving she hadn't even noticed? The thought made something twist inside her chest. She looked at her mother differently now. Not like a daughter but like someone assessing damage. Mikey started walking towards the fridge. Instinct pulled Marie's attention back to him immediately. She picked him up, resting him against her shoulder protectively.

"You hungry baby do you want a snack until dinner"

"Yes momma"

Behind her, Vicky froze briefly when he called Marie momma then quickly went back to scanning the kitchen. Looking for something. Not food, not water but something else. Marie saw it without turning and that was when she understood. Her mother hadn't come home because she missed them. She came home because she needed something again. And Marie, at 17 years old was still the one holding everything together.

The house felt smaller after that argument. Vicky moved around like nothing had happened. Like she hadn't just walked back into the apartment carrying another life she didn't plan to raise. Marie moved around like she hadn't just swallowed her anger whole. Mikey had just turned two a week before. Darnell had brought a small cupcake with blue frosting and a toy truck that made too much noise. Mikey had squealed and smeared frosting across his cheeks while Darnell laughed like the moment meant something real. For a second, it had felt like a family. Now the apartment felt tense again. Vicky's belly grew slowly over the next few weeks, impossible to ignore. She didn't speak about it. Marie didn't ask again. They moved around each other like strangers sharing space. Darnell noticed everything. He always did. He noticed Marie's exhaustion before she admitted it. He noticed when she skipped meals. He noticed when she stared too long at nothing. He also noticed something else.

"You good?" he asked one afternoon, watching her lean against the counter longer than usual.

"I'm fine."

"You ain't been eating."

"I eat."

"You push food around. That ain't eating."

She rolled her eyes.

"You sound like an old man."

He smirked faintly.

"Maybe I am."

She turned back to the stove, but the smell of the onions suddenly made her stomach twist.

She swallowed hard.

Darnell's eyes narrowed slightly.

"You sick?"

"No."

She wasn't sure if she was lying. The next few days, it happened again. She'd wake up feeling off, dizzy and tired in a different way not just exhaustion, heavy. Darnell caught her sitting on the couch one evening, staring at the wall while Mikey napped.

"You ain't been yourself."

"I'm fine."

He crouched in front of her, elbows resting on his knees.

"When your cycle supposed to come?"

Her heart skipped.

She looked at him sharply.

"Why you asking that?"

He didn't blink.

"Just answer."

She did the math in her head. Silence stretched. Her throat felt dry.

"...It's late."

"How late?"

She didn't answer.

He leaned back slowly.

A muscle in his jaw tightened.

"You pregnant?"

The word hit the air heavy.

She shook her head too fast.

"No."

"You sure?"

Her mind started racing. She thought about the last few weeks. The nausea, the fatigue. The way her body felt different. She felt heat crawl up her neck.

"I don't know."

The vulnerability in her voice surprised even her. Darnell stood up and started pacing the kitchen slowly, not angry just thinking.

"Why you ain't tell me?"

"I didn't even think about it."

He stopped walking and looked at her with intensity.

"If you are," he said quietly, "that's ours."

Something in her chest tightened. Not fear not yet, just weight. She looked toward Vicky's closed bedroom door instinctively. Two pregnant women in the same apartment two different futures. Her breath caught.

"What if I am?" she whispered.

He stepped closer again.

"You think I'm running?"

She didn't answer because she didn't know. He reached for her chin gently, lifting her face so she had to look at him.

"You think I'm built like that?"

She shook her head slowly, he leaned his forehead against hers.

"If you pregnant… that's my baby and we're keeping it."

The way he said it sounded like promise, like ownership, like inevitability, like she was wanted for once. And for a second, the chaos in her life felt like it might anchor instead of explode. But down the hall Vicky moved around the apartment carrying her own pregnancy like it was just another thing happening to her. And Marie felt something complicated blooming inside her, fear, hope. And the terrifying possibility that she might become her mother… before she ever fully stopped being her daughter.

It was a chill Sunday. The test sat on the bathroom sink between them. The apartment was quiet. Mikey was asleep downstairs with Mrs. Alvarez. Vicky hadn't been home in two days. Darnell had gone out and bought the test himself. He didn't ask her if she wanted him to. He just came back with it in a small plastic bag like it was something necessary. Like it was already decided.

"Take it babe," he said calmly.

Her hands trembled slightly as she did. They waited together. The bathroom felt too small. Too quiet. Too loud at the same time. Marie stared at the stick like it might change its mind. One line appeared. Her heart pounded. Then the second Pink, clear, unmistakable. For a split second, neither of them moved. Then Darnell let out a breath that sounded like a laugh and relief tangled together.

"I knew it," he said softly.

Before she could process anything, he lifted her up off the bathroom floor like she weighed nothing.

"We having a baby," he said into her hair.

He wasn't scared, he wasn't angry, he was happy. That was the part that made it easier for her to let herself smile too. He set her down and pulled her into his chest, kissing the top of her head, then her forehead, then her cheeks.

"That's my baby," he murmured. "You hear me? That's ours."

For a moment, she let herself sink into it. Into the feeling of being chosen. Into the feeling of building something that was hers. But somewhere in the back of her mind, something whispered. You already take care of one no you're about to take care of three. Because Vicky was still pregnant too. And Marie knew in a way that didn't need to be spoken that her mother wouldn't be raising this next child either. The first couple of months felt almost... beautiful. Darnell stepped in completely. He brought home bags of baby clothes before she even started showing. Tiny socks, onesies, blankets, diapers and more. And not just for her but for Vicky's baby too. "You ain't gotta worry about nothing," he told her over and over. He bought her whatever she needed. Cravings? Handled. Doctor's appointments? He drove her. Groceries? Already in the fridge. As her tiny belly began to curve outward, he would kneel in front of her, press his palm gently against it like he could already feel movement.

"That's mine," he'd say softly.

He kissed her stomach like it was sacred. Wrapped his arms around her from behind when she cooked, hands resting on her growing middle.

"You good?" he'd ask constantly.

And she was, or she convinced herself she was. He became even more present, more protective, More involved. And at first, the protectiveness felt like love.

"You don't need to be walking around by yourself," he told her one afternoon when she mentioned going to the store alone.

"I been doing it," she replied.

"Yeah, before."

Before what? He didn't have to say it.

"Before you was carrying my baby."

"I'll send one of my boys to grab what you need," he said casually. "You don't gotta be out there."

It sounded reasonable, It sounded safe so she agreed. Then it was, "Text me when you get to Mrs. Alvarez's." Then it was, "Why you ain't answer right away?"

Then it was, "You don't need to be standing outside talking to people."

She started noticing how often his eyes were on her. Even when he wasn't physically there.

Corner boys would nod when she walked past. Watching and reporting.

"Just protection," he'd say.

"For you and my baby."

And she let it slide. Because he still kissed her forehead at night. Still rubbed her belly, still laughed with Mikey, still brought groceries, still fixed things around the apartment and He was still loving. Just... tighter. Keisha came over one afternoon like she always had.

They were sitting on the couch laughing about some new guy she was messing with when Darnell walked in. His jaw tightened almost immediately. Later that night, he brought it up.

"I don't like her."

"Why?"

"She too loud, too fast she's a bad influence and ain't on your level."

"She's my friend."

"You got a baby coming," he said flatly. "You don't need people around you that don't move right."

She crossed her arms.

"She's been there for me and always has my back."

He stared at her for a long second.

"Pick better friends baby."

The next time Keisha tried to come over, Darnell made sure he was already there. The next time after that, he told Marie he didn't want her over anymore.

"She don't respect you."

It wasn't loud, it wasn't violent but it was firm. And Marie, tired and pregnant and balancing Mikey and Vicky's growing belly in the background, let it go. Small things always small at first.

"Don't smile like that at him."

"You don't need to be that friendly."

"Stay close to the house."

If she laughed too loud at something someone said outside, he'd snap quietly later.

"You think that's funny?"

And she'd blink at him, confused because he had never been like this. Not in the beginning but he still kissed her gently, still told her he loved her and he did. In his own warped, possessive way. But something had shifted. Before, she was his girl. Now, she was carrying his child. And somewhere in his mind, that made her his completely, property not partner. And she didn't fully see it yet. Because the love still felt real. And love, when it comes wrapped in protection and provision, is hard to question. Vicky's pregnancy progressed the way everything else in her life did. Half acknowledged and half-carried. She didn't go to appointments regularly she didn't count weeks out loud, didn't talk about names or fold baby clothes but Marie did. Not just because she wanted to but because she knew no one else would. By the time Vicky's belly was heavy and low, Marie's was beginning to lower & firm too. The sight of it unsettled her sometimes two pregnant bodies moving through the same narrow hallway like mirrored warnings. One afternoon Vicky stood in the kitchen rubbing her lower back.

"It's starting," she muttered.

Marie looked up immediately.

"What's starting?"

Vicky didn't answer. She just gripped the counter tighter.

The contraction hit visibly this time. Marie's heart started racing. Darnell wasn't home yet. Mikey was playing on the floor with a truck, Marie moved fast.

"Sit down," she said firmly, guiding Vicky toward the couch. As always, their roles reversed completely. Marie grabbed her phone and called Darnell.

"She in labor," she said.

"I'm on my way."

He didn't hesitate. The ride to the hospital was quiet except for Vicky's strained breathing and Marie's constant checking.

"You good? You need water? You okay?"

Vicky barely responded.

At the hospital, everything felt too bright.

Marie held her mother's hand through contractions even though part of her wanted to pull away. Nurses moved around them efficiently. Questions were asked.

"Father?"

Vicky didn't answer.

Marie didn't either, honestly she never even asked her mother who the father was. Hours later, Melanie was born. Tiny, Red-faced, crying strong. Marie stood at the foot of the hospital bed watching her sister enter the world. Vicky looked at the baby for a moment. Just a moment, no tears, no glow just… exhaustion. The nurse handed Melanie to Marie first while Vicky closed her eyes. Marie held her carefully, staring down at her tiny features.

"You're perfect," she whispered.

And she meant it. They brought Melanie home two days later and for the first few weeks, Vicky stayed. That surprised Marie. She would sit on the couch holding the baby. Feed her, rock her and bathe her, not consistently but enough to make Marie think maybe this time would be different. Until her disappearing started again. By this time, Marie and Darnell weren't surprised anymore they let her come in when she needed and see the baby. She would stay when she wanted and leave when she did. Darnell helped more. He fixed a small crib, changed diapers, made sure formula never ran low. Sometimes he would stand behind Marie while she held both Mikey and Melanie and just watch her quietly.

"You built for this," he said once.

She didn't know if that was a compliment.

Life, strangely, began to feel structured, not easy never easy but structured.

Mikey had just turned three. He followed Darnell everywhere now, tiny sneakers slapping the floor behind him. Melanie was three months old, round-cheeked and alert, watching everything like she was already trying to understand the world she'd been dropped into. And Marie… Marie was heavy. Her belly was swollen and low, stretched tight and full. Every step felt slower. Her back ached constantly. She couldn't see her own feet anymore. Sometimes she'd stand in the kitchen with one hand pressed against her lower spine and just breathe through the exhaustion. Three, Three babies. A three year old, three month old and one ready to drop any day. She was terrified, she didn't say it often but at night, when Darnell wrapped his arms around her from behind, she'd whisper it into the dark.

"I don't know how I'm gonna do this."

He'd press his palm over her belly gently.

"You ain't doing it alone."

And even though he wasn't perfect even though he was flawed, rough around the edges, still learning softness he had shown up in ways no one else ever had. He worked even if it was the streets, he still provided the only way he knew how. He woke up when they cried, he changed diapers, he rocked Melanie when she refused to sleep. He took Mikey and Melanie outside so Marie could nap. They made a decision quietly one afternoon, no more in and out for Vicky. The bedroom that once belonged to her was cleaned out. Darnell carried old clothes, broken furniture, and whatever remnants of her presence remained down the stairs without commentary. They turned it into a nursery temporary, he said.

"As soon as you drop," he told Marie, standing in the doorway looking at the freshly assembled crib, "we looking at houses. You deserve more than this apartment." The only thing that had ever stopped him before was Vicky. And now… That wasn't happening anymore. He refused to see Marie hurting every time Vicky walked out that door. One night, they were eating takeout from Preciosa's. Their favorite place. A little Chinese-Spanish mix spot on the corner with neon lights that never fully worked. Darnell loved their fried rice with pernil. Marie always ordered lo mein with maduros on the side. Mikey was half asleep on the couch, Melanie rested in Darnell's arms, her tiny hand gripping his shirt. Marie took a slow sip of her iced tea, grateful for the brief calm. Then came the knock. Darnell shifted slightly.

"I'll get it."

"You got Mel," Marie said gently. "I got it, baby."

She stood slowly, one hand under her belly out of habit, iced tea still in her other hand.

She walked to the door.

Something in her chest tightened before she even opened it. She didn't know why she just felt it, she pulled the door open. Two officers stood there, for a split second, time bent. Déjà vu hit her so hard it felt physical. The hallway, the uniforms, the stillness just like when Mitch died.

"Are you the family of a Victoria Lopez?" one officer asked carefully.

Behind her, Darnell called out, "Baby, who is it?"

But Marie didn't hear him.

The words blurred. The hallway seemed to tilt, her iced tea slipped from her hand spilling against the floor. Ice scattering, liquid spreading she couldn't feel her fingers anymore.

The officer kept speaking but she only hear him in increments.

"...found earlier this evening..."

"...suspected overdose..."

"...we're sorry..."

Darnell was already moving.

He placed Melanie gently into the playpen without panic instinctively, efficiently and walked toward the door. He saw Marie's face just as her knees began to weaken. He caught her before she fell, always right on time. He wrapped one arm around her waist and guided her backward.

"Sit down," he murmured quietly.

He handled the officers from there, answered questions, confirmed identity, nodded when necessary. Marie sat on the edge of the couch staring at nothing. Her ears rang. A mix of feelings flooded her all at once, a sadness sharp and sudden. The little girl in her who remembered Sunday mornings getting her hair braided and Whitney songs, was crying out somewhere deep inside. Hurt, because no matter how much anger she carried, that was still her mother. And then relief, quiet and unspoken. The breath she had been holding for years finally released. No more wondering when the knock would come or waiting for her mother to get clean. That last fragile thread of hope snapped and with it, the waiting ended. Tears slid down her face silently. Darnell came back inside after closing the door. He knelt in front of her. She looked at him like she was seeing him from far away.

"She's gone," she whispered.

He nodded slowly and that's when it happened. A warmth spread suddenly between her legs. Slow at first then undeniable. Marie's eyes widened she looked down. Water pooled beneath her. Darnell followed her gaze. For a second neither of them spoke. Then he looked back up at her, calm but alert.

"Your water broke."

Everything had collided at once, death, grief, relief and life beginning. Marie let out a shaky breath.

"Of course it did," she whispered.

And Darnell stood up immediately, already moving, already thinking, already steady.

"Okay," he said softly.

"Okay I'm calling Ms. Alvarez, We going to the hospital."

And in that moment with two children in the apartment and another about to arrive he did not look like a boy from the block. He looked like a father. The hospital lights felt harsher this time. Marie lay in the bed gripping the rails while nurses moved quickly around her. Contractions came stronger now sharp, deep waves that stole her breath mid sentence. Darnell stood beside her, steady. He wasn't pacing or panicking he was watching her. Every breath she took, every wince, every tremble.

"You good baby," he murmured, brushing hair from her forehead.

She nodded even though she wasn't. In between contractions, her mind drifted. Her mother was gone. While she was bringing life into the world, the woman who brought her into it had just left it. It felt cruel and poetic. It felt like something bigger than her. Another contraction hit. She squeezed Darnell's hand so hard her knuckles turned white.

"You so strong baby," he whispered.

And for once, she didn't roll her eyes at that word. Because right now, she had no choice but to be. Hours later, with sweat on her brow and tears on her cheeks not all from pain the room filled with the sharp cry of new life, a girl. The nurse lifted her gently. Tiny, pink and most importantly alive.

"Dad?" the nurse asked.

Darnell stepped forward slowly. He had seen babies before, held Mikey, held Melanie but this was different, this was his. He cut the umbilical cord and when they placed her into his arms, something in his chest cracked open in a way he didn't expect. She was small, so small. Her fingers curled instinctively around his thumb and that was it. He exhaled slowly. His throat tightened. His eyes softened in a way Marie had never seen before.

"This my baby girl," he said under his breath. Not possessive, not territorial just in awe, pure awe. He looked at Marie, really looked at her. Her hair damp, face tired her eyes shining with tears. And something washed over him that wasn't control, it was gratitude.

"You did this," he said quietly.

She gave him a faint smile.

"We did."

He shook his head slightly.

"No baby," he said, voice thick. "You carried her, you brought her here."

He stepped closer to the bed and gently lowered the baby into Marie's arms. But he didn't let go completely. His hand stayed under the baby's back, supporting them both.

"You gave her life," he said softly. "You gave me her."

And Marie saw it, the shift. The way he looked at his daughter wasn't the way he looked at ownership. It was the way someone looks at something sacred.

"What you wanna name her?" Marie asked gently.

She let him, she wanted him to. He stared at the baby for a long moment.

"She's mine," he murmured again. Then he looked at Marie.

"Amara," he said slowly.

Marie's eyes softened.

"Amara."

He nodded.

"It means grace."

He leaned down and pressed his lips to his daughter's forehead, then to Marie's. And in that hospital room with grief still fresh and life just beginning Darnell fell in love in a way he didn't know he was capable of. The kind that makes a man realize he has something to lose. He looked at Amara again, then at Marie, and a thought settled heavy in his chest. One day, this little girl is going to look at me to learn what love looks like. One day, she's going to choose a man and I never want her to think control is love. He didn't say it out loud, not yet. But it planted something, something that would grow.

The house was loud in a new way, three children changed the atmosphere. Mikey was testing boundaries, Melanie was teething and Amara awoke every two hours like clockwork. Marie hadn't slept more than ninety minutes straight in weeks. Her body was still healing, her hormones were still crashing and rising like waves and her patience was thin. Darnell tried, he really did. He woke up for bottles, he rocked Amara at night and kept the house stocked. But the streets still called him, and sometimes the weight of providing for five people pressed heavy on his shoulders.

One afternoon, one of his boys stopped by, Not unusual although he tried to keep business outside. They were in the living room talking low about something business related. Mikey sat on the floor with toy cars, Melanie napped in the playpen. Marie had finally fallen asleep in the bedroom with Amara beside her. For the first time all day, the apartment felt quiet. Then Amara cried, Sharp and hungry Marie jolted awake, disoriented. She didn't check herself in the mirror or look down at herself she didn't think. She grabbed Amara quickly and walked out of the bedroom in a loose tank top that had slipped low from nursing and sleep. No bra. No awareness just pure mother instinct. She stepped into the living room half asleep. Darnell's boy looked up. Just for a second, long enough to see her exposed, his eyes lingered just for a moment but long enough for Darnell to see it. Something in him snapped fast. He stood up immediately.

"Get out," he told his boy sharply.

"Bro—"

"I said get out."

His tone left no room for argument, The door closed behind him, followed by silence. Marie blinked, confused, still adjusting Amara in her arms, she noticed the look on Darnell's face.

"What—"

Before she finished, Darnell crossed the room. He grabbed her, his hand came up under her jaw, gripping at her neck as he pulled her toward him.

"Why you walking out like that?" he snapped.

It wasn't a choke but it was forceful. Enough to shock her and enough to hurt her, Amara let out a startled cry between them. Marie froze, not because of pain but because of the look in his eyes. Anger, Possession, Humiliation. Her own eyes filled instantly not loud crying, not screaming just stunned, confused and hurt.

"I didn't" she started softly. "I didn't know he was here."

Her voice shook, Darnell's grip tightened for half a second Then he saw it. The fear in her face, the way her shoulders curled inward. The way she instinctively tried to protect the baby in her arms. And something inside him dropped. His hand loosened immediately. He stepped back like he'd just touched fire. Marie didn't yell, she didn't curse, she didn't swing at him. She just looked at him, and that look that quiet, wounded, exhausted look hit him harder than anything else could have. She adjusted her tank top slowly, shifted Amara higher against her chest.

"I was asleep," she said softly. "I didn't even think."

Her voice wasn't challenging, it wasn't dramatic, it was broken and tired.

"You think I'd disrespect you?" she whispered.

That question landed heavier than the grab because he knew the answer... No, she wouldn't, she never had. She had dropped out of school. Given him loyalty, carried his child, built his home, fed him, trusted him, and loved him. And he had just put his hands on her like she was something to control. He looked at Amara so tiny and innocent. One day, this little girl is going to look at me to learn what love looks like. The thought didn't come gently it came like a warning. He imagined someone grabbing her like that. His jaw tightened and his stomach turned. He stepped back further, hands lifting slightly like he didn't trust them.

"I..." His voice faltered.

He wasn't good with apologies. He was good with money, with protection, with presence, not softness. Marie was the first person to ever bring out any kind of softness in him.

"I ain't mean to..." he started. Marie shook her head slightly.

"Don't," she said quietly.

Not dismissive, just overwhelmed and hurt. She walked past him slowly and went back into the bedroom. Not slamming the door, no screaming, not dramatic just closing it. And that silence was louder than anything she could have said. Darnell stood in the living room alone his chest tight his hands still warm from where they'd grabbed her. He walked to the bathroom mirror and stared at himself. He didn't see a provider, he didn't see a protector. He saw a man who almost became the thing he hated, His father. He saw the kind of man he never wanted his daughter to choose. And something in him shifted that day. For the first time, he was afraid of really losing her and everything they've built together. Inside the bedroom, Marie sat on the edge of the bed nursing Amara. Her neck wasn't bruised just red, his finger marks still lingering but her heart was bruised. She didn't cry loudly or dramatically just let silent tears fall while she looked at her daughter.

"I won't let you live around that" she whispered softly.

And she meant it. Darnell didn't knock on the bedroom door. He stood outside it for a long time first. Inside, Marie had both babies with her. Melanie in the playpen near the bed. Amara against her chest. Mikey already tucked in his little bed down the hall. The apartment felt heavy, Darnell moved quietly through it, he checked on Mikey first. Pulled the blanket up over his small shoulders, brushed a hand over his head. Then he grabbed his keys to go get some air. He drove without his usual music, windows cracked. The city lights blurred past him, he replayed it over and over. Her face. The way her body curled inward. The way she asked, "You think I'd disrespect you?" He had grown up watching men yell before they spoke. Watching hands move faster than words. Watching control mistaken for love. Most importantly, he watched his father abuse his mother, watched how after a beating his mother would turn to drugs for escape. No one had ever shown him how to be gentle. He had learned how to provide, how to fight, how to protect territory but not how to protect a heart or a woman. He pulled over at a red light and gripped the steering wheel tight. He imagined someone grabbing Amara like that one day and his stomach turned again.

"I ain't that," he muttered to himself.

But tonight, he had been and that scared him. When he came back, the apartment was quiet. He stood outside the bedroom door again. This time, he knocked softly.

"Marie."

Silence. Then, "Come in."

She was sitting against the headboard, Melanie asleep in her playpen beside her, Amara tucked in her arms. She looked tired and hurt, fresh tears on her cheeks. He stepped inside slowly and closed the door behind him. For a moment, he didn't speak. He sat on the edge of the bed, leaving space between them.

"I went to think," he said quietly.

She nodded once. He ran a hand down his face.

"I don't know how to do this."

She looked at him finally.

"Do what."

"Be this."

He gestured vaguely around the room.

"A man, a father, a husband one day, I ain't grow up seeing it done right."

His voice wasn't defensive, it wasn't loud, it was stripped down.

"I seen control," he continued. "I seen yelling, screaming and fighting. It was always hands first, words later. I thought that's what you do when you scared of losing something." I saw abuse I saw how my dad would beat my mom and kiss her later. How he would tell her he would never do it again and he didn't want to lose her. I always told myself I would never be like him and tonight scared me.

Marie's eyes softened slightly.

He swallowed.

"When I saw him look at you..." he admitted, "I felt stupid, I felt small, Like I ain't enough."

She didn't interrupt.

"I grabbed you because I was scared," he said. "Not because you did anything, because I ain't never had something that mattered this much and I was wrong to do that to you baby."

Silence settled between them.

"I would never disrespect you," she said gently.

"I know," he whispered.

His voice cracked just slightly.

"That's what messed me up, I know you wouldn't."

He looked at Amara sleeping peacefully against her chest.

"I don't ever want her thinking that's love," he said quietly.

That hit her hard.

He looked back at Marie.

“And I don’t ever want you looking at me like that again. I don’t ever wanna cause you pain”

Her throat tightened. He shifted closer, cautiously, like approaching something fragile.

“I’m so sorry,” he said.

And for a man like him, that was everything. Marie felt tears slip down her face. She shifted slightly, laying Amara down in the bassinet beside her. She gently pulled him closer. He rested his head against her chest, like a child, like someone who finally stopped fighting. Her fingers moved into his hair automatically. They sat like that for a long time, just breathing. The babies slept softly around them.

“I’m tired too,” she whispered into his hair.

“I know,” he said.

“I don’t ever want to be scared of you.”

His body went still.

“You won’t be,” he said.

Not as a threat but as a promise. They lay down slowly after that, quietly, closely, with gentleness. The kind of closeness that comes after truth. He kissed her softly, not demanding, just gentle. She kissed him back and when they came together, they made love it wasn’t fire. It was reconnection, soft intentional and slow reminding each other they were still there. Afterward, they lay tangled in silence, listening to the rhythm of their daughter’s breathing. Darnell’s arm rested gently around her not tight or restrictive because although they just made love, he still had that look of fear in her eyes embedded in his mind.

The morning after nothing in the apartment looked different but the air between them felt different. Darnell moved quieter that morning. Not distant just careful. Like he didn't want to disturb the fragile thing they'd rebuilt in the dark. Marie woke to him in the kitchen making bottles with the focus of someone trying to do it right. He didn't say much. Just glanced at her and asked, "You okay?" She nodded once. And for the first time in a long time, she meant it. Vicky's death sat in the background like a low hum. It didn't scream every moment, but it was always there. In the silence of her old room. In the way Marie sometimes caught herself listening for footsteps that would never come back. Darnell handled what needed handling because Marie couldn't. They didn't do a funeral, not because Vicky didn't matter but because there was no one to fill a room. No aunties calling, no cousins arriving no old family friends. It was Just them and the kids. Just the reality that Vicky had lived and disappeared in the same way she lived. So they chose cremation, quiet simple and private. Marie signed papers with hands that didn't feel like her own while Darnell stood beside her like a wall steady, present and not letting her fold.

Weeks later, when the ashes came back in a small sealed container, Marie stared at it too long. This... is all that's left? That thought broke something open in her. Darnell didn't rush her he just said, "What you wanna do with her?" Marie swallowed.

"I don't want her... gone gone."

So they did something that felt like a compromise between grief and survival.

They ordered three small keepsake necklaces. Nothing flashy just simple chains with tiny heart capsules that could hold a bit of ash. One for Marie, one for Mikey and one for Melanie. Marie held the necklaces in her palm at the kitchen table when they arrived, the chains tangling together like a quiet symbol.

"She didn't give them much," Marie whispered.

Darnell sat across from her, watching her without interrupting.

"But I don't want them to grow up thinking they came from nothing," she continued. "Even if she was... what she was... she's still our mother."

He nodded slowly.

"You gonna give it to them when they're older?"

Marie nodded.

"When they can understand and when it won't feel like a curse."

She slipped her own necklace on first, the heart capsule rested against her chest. She exhaled shakily and pressed her palm over it. For the first time since the officers stood in her hallway, she cried in a way that didn't feel like shock, just grief. Darnell reached across the table and held her hand. That was his new love language learning when silence was the safest thing to offer. After that, Darnell started changing in ways that didn't come with announcements. It wasn't a grand declaration like, I'm done with the streets, it was smaller. He stopped staying out late "just because." He stopped taking certain calls in front of her. He started coming home with a different look in his eyes like his mind was somewhere else. He was planning and building something.

One night, Marie found him sitting at the table with a notebook open, writing numbers down.

"What's that?" she asked.

Darnell looked up like he'd been caught.

"Just a little something I'm working on for us."

She raised an eyebrow. "Something like what?"

He sighed like he didn't know how to say it without sounding foolish.

"A way out," he said finally.

Marie blinked. "Out?"

He nodded once.

"I can't be doing this forever," he admitted quietly. "Not with them and not with you."

He glanced toward the bedroom where the kids were asleep Mikey sprawled sideways on their bed, Melanie tucked tight, Amara's little chest rising and falling.

"I don't want them growing up watching me disappear," he said. "Or watching me be a drug dealer my whole life, or worse dead or in jail like my pops."

Marie's throat tightened.

"Then don't," she whispered.

He looked back at the notebook.

"I been thinking about music," he said. "How everybody out here has something to say but nowhere to go that's safe. I could build something, a studio, a real one not some backroom."

Marie stared at him.

"You serious?"

He nodded. "I'm dead serious."

He said it with conviction the kind that scared him a little too...

The first time he took Marie to see the space, it was just a dusty storefront with old posters still taped to the window. But Darnell stood in the middle of it like he could already hear the beat.

"Right here," he said, pointing. "Soundproof booth."

He walked a few steps. "Right here, the lounge for the young ones, snacks, drinks, games a safe spot."

Marie smiled. "You got a whole vision baby."

He glanced at her. "You the one who taught me how to build a home."

That hit her deep because she had built a home her whole life out of scraps. Now he was building one out of purpose. He named it something meaningful something that was his, Legacy. A company that wasn't just about profit. It was about giving kids the thing he never had, guidance without harm. Where established artist would pay for their sessions and he'd give the young ones free sessions. If they were doing good in school and doing right, he'd do right by them. And little by little, the streets loosened their grip on him. Not because they stopped calling but because Darnell stopped answering like he used to.

Three years passed, but not in a blur, in moments. Mikey started kindergarten. Melanie learned to talk in full sentences, her voice bright and bossy. Amara grew into Darnell's shadow always reaching for him, always lighting up when he walked into a room.

Marie turned twenty-one, Darnell turned twenty-three. And one morning, Marie stood at the window of a house outside the city real grass, real driveway, trees that didn't grow out of sidewalk cracks and she felt like she was watching someone else's life. Mikey was six, Melanie and Amara were three. Darnell came up behind her, hands resting gently on her waist.

"You like it?" he asked.

Marie laughed softly, overwhelmed. "Like it?" she whispered. "Darnell... this is something I used to see on TV." He kissed the side of her head.

"This ours," he said. "You earned this."

And she realized she wasn't holding her breath anymore.

Marie went back to school with a hunger that surprised even her because she suddenly had time and support. The girls went to daycare in the mornings, hair in neat little styles Marie insisted on even if she was rushing. Mikey went to school with a full lunch and a clean backpack. And Marie... Marie sat in classrooms again, older than most students, tired but determined. She became a 911 dispatcher because it was the closest thing to purpose she could touch immediately while in school. Something steady, something meaningful, something that made her feel like her life had turned into fuel instead of damage.

Her first weeks on the job shook her. She'd come home quiet sometimes, sitting at the kitchen table staring into nothing. Darnell would slide a plate in front of her.

"You ate?" he'd ask.

"I will babe."

He'd sit beside her, not pushing her to talk, just there. And slowly, she started telling him about the calls. The fear in people's voices, the way seconds mattered, the way a calm voice could save a life. One night, she said it out loud like a secret.

"I think I want to be a social worker."

Darnell looked at her, eyebrows lifting.

"A social worker?"

Marie nodded, almost shy.

"I want to help people... before it gets to 911. Before it's too late. I want to protect girls like me and help women like our mothers."

He didn't laugh or doubt her he just leaned back and smiled slow.

"Then you gonna be one," he said.

And somehow, hearing him say it made it feel possible.

The proposal happened on a night that looked ordinary from the outside. Kids asleep, house quiet one of her favorite songs playing low Love by Musiq Soulchild. It reminded her of Sundays before her mom got addicted, memories. Marie walked into the living room and stopped. Candles were lit enough to make the walls glow warm like the house itself was exhaling. A small table had been set up with food from Preciosa's with her favorite order. The same thing she used to get when they barely knew each other but somehow knew each other perfectly. On the couch sat three tiny boxes. Marie's heart started beating fast not just from surprise, but from deep gratitude, this felt intentional. Darnell stepped in from the kitchen wearing a clean button down. The kind you only wore to court dates or job interviews, his hands were slightly shaking. He didn't speak right away. He just stood in front of her, looking at her like a man staring at something sacred. Like he was trying to memorize her face in case the world ever tried to take it from him. "I don't know how to do fancy baby," he said softly.

Marie let out a shaky breath. "Well You're doing it babe."

He nodded, but his jaw tightened. Something deeper was sitting on his chest.

"I grew up thinking love was rough," he said. "Doors slamming, voices raised, men leaving and in the streets, women surviving."

Marie's throat tightened.

"I thought love meant you grab tight, you hold hard. You don't let nobody breathe because you scared they'll disappear."

He looked down at his hands.

"I watched men live the street life, I watched women cry, I watched kids grow up too fast and I was in the middle of it all."

His voice dropped lower.

"And I promised myself I'd never be that man."

He looked up at her now.

"But I didn't know how to be different, so I repeated the cycle."

Marie's eyes were glassy.

"You," he said, pointing gently at her chest, "you grew up fighting too. You lost people before you even understood what loss meant. You carried siblings on your back when you were still a child, you loved children when you barely got to be one."

Her breath trembled.

"You buried people you shouldn't have had to bury. You learned how to survive before you ever learned how to rest."

A tear slid down her cheek.

"And somehow," he continued, "you still love soft, you still love patient, you still love like it ain't ever been broken."

His voice cracked just slightly.

"You made me understand that love ain't possession, it ain't control and it ain't fear."

He stepped closer.

“It’s staying, it’s fighting for each other, it’s protecting what you love, it’s showing up even on those hard days.”

His thumb brushed her knuckles.

“It’s coming home.”

He swallowed hard.

“It’s building something so steady our kids don’t even know what chaos feels like.”

He took her hands fully now.

“I want Amara to grow up never questioning if a man will choose her.”

His voice thickened.

“I want Mikey to know strength ain’t about anger. It’s about protection.”

“And I want Melanie to know she don’t have to be strong all the time. That somebody’s always gonna be strong for her too.”

Marie was crying openly now.

He slowly lowered himself to one knee.

“I ain’t perfect,” he said. “I still got scars I still got pride I’m learning to lay down. But I wake up every day choosing to be better than the boy I used to be.”

He looked up at her like she was his compass.

“And I want to spend the rest of my life proving to you that loving you was the best decision I ever made.”

He gestured to the couch.

“I’m not just asking you to be my wife.”

He opened the first box. The ring caught the candlelight simple, beautiful, steady.

"I'm asking you to build with me."

Second box, A bracelet engraved with Mikey's name.

Third, Melanie's.

And then he reached into his pocket and pulled out one more.

Amara's.

"I want my name tied to theirs legally," he said. "I want paperwork to match my heart. I want us to adopt them. I want every teacher, every doctor, every form to know they're ours."

His voice broke fully now.

"Because I chose them."

He looked at her through tears he wasn't hiding anymore.

"And Marie… I chose you."

A breath, a whisper.

"I choose you on your worst days. On the tired ones, on the days you doubt yourself, on the days you think you too much or not enough." He shook his head.

"You're everything."

Silence filled the room but it wasn't empty, It was full.

"So baby," he whispered, voice barely holding steady, "will you marry me? Will you let me spend the rest of my life giving you and our kids the life we never had?"

Marie dropped to her knees in front of him. Pressed her forehead to his.

"Yes," she breathed. "Yes."

And for a moment it was just them. Two kids who grew up way too fast but finally choosing to slow down.

Then a tiny voice from the hallway.

"...Mama?"

They both froze.

Marie turned.

Mikey was standing there in the dim light, hair messy from sleep, rubbing one eye. He must've woken up from the music. He looked between them, then at Darnell on one knee.

"Why you on the floor Dee?" he asked like any typical curious kid.

Darnell let out a wet laugh through his tears. Marie smiled, reaching her hand out. "Come here, baby." Mikey hesitated for half a second like he was trying to understand what he walked into. Then he strode across the floor, Darnell didn't stand up he stayed on his knee.

Because this mattered to him. He opened his arms.

"C'mere, little man."

Mikey stepped into them, small arms wrapping around Darnell's neck, And that was it. That was the moment Darnell broke, he hugged him tight.

"I was actually waiting for you," Darnell murmured into his hair.

Mikey pulled back. "For me?"

Darnell reached over to the couch and grabbed one of the boxes.

"This one's yours."

Mikey's eyes widened. Darnell opened it slowly.

Inside was the bracelet chunkier than the others. Solid and strong.

"For me?" Mikey whispered.

"For you," Darnell nodded. "Because you ain't just a kid I help with."

He swallowed.

"You my son and I'm your abba, abba means father in Hebrew."

"Abba" Mikey smiled and whispered.

Marie covered her mouth again.

Darnell slid the bracelet onto Mikey's wrist carefully, adjusting it so it fit just right.

"I made sure yours was different," he said softly. "A little heavier."

Mikey looked up at him. "Why?"

Darnell rested his forehead against Mikey's.

"Because you the little man of this house."

Mikey blinked.

Darnell continued, voice steady but thick.

"You next in charge after me. That means you protect your sisters. You respect your mama. You lead with kindness. And you never, ever run from responsibility."

Mikey nodded like he understood more than his age allowed.

"And guess what else, we want to adopt you and Melanie officially"

"You gonna adopt me for real?" Mikey asked, almost scared to hope.

Darnell didn't hesitate.

"Yeah," he said. "For real, papers and everything, you all gonna have my last name, my protection, my promise for life."

He glanced up at Marie, then back at Mikey.

"And your mama?" he added gently. "She's been your mama since the first night she stayed up with you. Since the first time she packed your lunch and braided Melanie's hair before school. Since she chose y'all before anybody asked her to."

Marie's breath caught and Darnell's voice softened.

"She's been your mother in every way that counts. We just making it official on paper so the world can catch up to what we already know."

Mikey looked at Marie.

"Like... she's really my mom now?"

Marie dropped back down to her knees, pulling him close.

"I been your mom, baby," she whispered into his hair. "I just never needed a document to prove it."

Mikey's small hands grabbed her shirt.

"Then why we doing papers?"

Darnell crouched back down in front of him.

"Because," he said carefully, "when you choose somebody, you don't halfway choose them. You stand up and say it out loud. You protect it, you put your name on it. You make sure nobody can ever question it."

He looked at Marie when he said it.

"And I'm choosing all of you."

Mikey's lip trembled.

"So we all gonna have the same last name?"

"If that's what you want," Marie said softly.

Mikey nodded hard.

"Yeah. I want that."

Darnell smiled the kind of smile that comes from somewhere deep.

"Then that's what we doing."

He squeezed Mikey's shoulder gently.

"You my son. And she's your mama. Not because we had to be but because we wanted to be."

Mikey stepped forward and wrapped both of them in a hug, his bracelet cool against Darnell's neck. Marie closed her eyes because she had carried these children that weren't born from her body and loved them so fiercely it changed her. And now... She was being chosen too. Not just as a wife but as a mother, officially, publicly and permanently. Darnell pressed his forehead to both of theirs.

"Family ain't just blood," he murmured.

"It's who stays."

And that night the house felt different because love wasn't surviving there anymore. It was rooted because that house didn't just hold survival anymore, it held love and legacy.

They didn't want a big wedding. They had already survived enough drama in their lives. So they chose City Hall, something simple but intentional. The morning of, Marie wore a white dress that fell just below her knees. Nothing flashy, just classy and elegant. Her hair down pin straight, the small gold heart chain with her mothers ashes around her neck the only jewelry she needed besides her ring. Darnell wore a fitted suit, no tie he said he wanted to look like himself, not like somebody else's version of a groom. Mikey wore a little blazer that made him stand taller than usual. Melanie and Amara had matching cream dresses, their bracelets glinting on tiny wrists. Keisha stood beside Marie, not by chance but by growth. There was a time when her presence wouldn't have been possible when everything was too fresh, too messy, too unhealed. But time had done what time does when people are willing... it softened what once felt sharp. Darnell didn't just let Keisha back in. He watched and paid attention. To him just like they grew, her growth had to be real... not spoken. And when he saw it, when he saw she wasn't the same, when her energy came back different, quieter, more grounded he allowed space for her again. Not the same way, but in a way that made sense. And Marie... Marie never held onto pride when peace was an option. She had learned that some things aren't about who was right... they're about who is different now. So Keisha stood beside her. Not as who she used to be but as who she chose to become. On Darnell's side stood Jamal. His day one, the one who knew him before any of this... before the discipline, before the growth, before he figured out how to be a man instead of just surviving like one. They came from the same circle, the same streets. The same kind of nights that taught you how to move before you ever learned how to feel. Jamal had seen every version of him, the reckless one, the guarded one, the one who didn't trust nothing good to last. And now... this one. The man standing still, choosing something real.

City Hall was quiet. Fluorescent lights, neutral walls, nothing about it looked special. But when they stood in front of that clerk it felt sacred. Not because of the place… but because of what it took to get there. Darnell didn't look at the clerk when it was time. He looked at Marie.

"I choose you," he said, voice rough, but steady. "And I don't say that like it's easy… cause it's not. I ain't grow up seeing love done right. I seen what it looks like when it's broken… when it hurts more than it heals." He let that sit for a second.

"I had to learn everything the hard way. How to trust it how to stand in it how not to run when it get real."

His eyes stayed on hers.

"But you… you never ran. Even when you had every reason to. You been strong for everybody… carrying stuff people don't even see… and you still got love in you."

He shook his head slightly, almost in disbelief.

"That's rare. And I'm not taking that lightly."

A breath.

"I'm not here to fix you and I don't need you to fix me. But I am here to stand with you… to grow with you… to do this right, even when it ain't easy."

His voice dropped, but it hit deeper.

"I choose you, all of you. Every version you had to be just to get here."

Marie didn't cry, not this time. She felt it but she also felt this sense of calmness and certainty.

"I choose you too," she said, calm, but full. "And not because I need you… I've already learned how to stand on my own."

She stepped just a little closer.

"But I've also learned... that being strong doesn't mean doing everything alone."

Her eyes held his.

"You see me, not just what I give... but what I've been through to still be able to give it."

A breath left her, softer now.

"And you never made me feel like I had to hide that... or carry it by myself."

She smiled with a certainty.

"I trust you and you know how hard that is for me, I love you and I choose to build something real with you... not perfect... but honest and beautiful."

When the clerk pronounced them husband and wife it didn't feel like a beginning. It felt like something that had already been decided finally being spoken out loud. Mikey clapped first loud and proud. "Does that mean we officially a family now abba?" he asked. Darnell looked at him, a small smile breaking through.

"We been a family son."

Then he glanced back at Marie.

"Now it's just official."

Afterward, they went to dinner a long wooden table at Preciosa's. They toasted not just to marriage But to Marie. Her associate's degree had come in the mail the week before. Late nights studying at the kitchen table, typing papers between daycare pickups, highlighting textbooks while stirring rice and beans on the stove. Darnell stood up at dinner and tapped his glass.

"I married a wife today," he said, looking at her with quiet pride. "But I also married a woman who don't quit."

He raised his glass.

"To my baby Marie, Associate's degree earned, bachelor's on the way. And the first social worker our block ever gonna produce. She did that," he said simply. "While raising kids, while building a home, while holding me accountable."

He looked at her.

"And she ain't done."

Marie smiled softly, Everyone clapped, Marie laughed, embarrassed but glowing. That night, when they put the kids to bed, the house felt settled. Like something had clicked into place. And then Life kept moving.

Weeks after City Hall, after the celebration, after the clinking of glasses. After Marie hung her associate's degree on the wall she started researching bachelor's programs. Life felt steady and beautiful. Until the call that changed their lives forever...

www.ingramcontent.com/pod-product-compliance
Lightning Source LLC
LaVergne TN
LVHW090533110826
845146LV00003B/1082

* 9 7 9 8 9 9 4 2 3 8 3 1 8 *